The Idiot
Family on Holiday

by A.J.Stairmand

Enjoy the book

A Stairmand

ISBN: 978-1-9164503-0-1
A CIP catalogue record for this book is available
from the British Library.

Cover Illustration & Book Design by: Jonathan Gay

Published by: Stairmand Publishing 2019

Printed & Distributed by: York Publishing Services
64 Hallfield Road, Layerthorpe, York YO31 7ZQ

Acknowledgements

I would like to thank Jon Gay
for the dramatic front cover,
it epitomises the main character very well.
I would also like to add
my appreciation to Jon for the time taken
to layout the book.
I found the company, The Book Specialist's
advice invaluable and their thorough editing
of the text with many suggestions,
has improved the overall story.

Finally, I would like to thank family
and friends for constant support,
advice and encouragement, especially,
my late father, whose unfailing enthusiasm
and belief never faltered.

Dedication

To Michael, James, Will and my late, darling father.

Thank you

Books by the same author

Series

The Idiot Family at Home

Other books

Desmond's Dragon

Archie Dingletrotter's Flying Caravan

*Petronella Pumpernickel-Pinkstocking Berck
and Big Wart*

The Phantom Sock Snatcher

Chapter 1

The gold speckled, super duper yacht was stuck in the Thames. Staring up at the bright blue sky, Jimmelta sighed at the endless sunshine – there was just never a flood when you needed one! Peering down her gold tinted periscope at the chaos below, she saw a mixture of soldiers and marines, trying to move the hulk, but with little success. Jimmelta just couldn't understand and frowned.

Weren't these the men who protected her

country to keep it safe?

If so, what was wrong with moving her 'little' yacht down the river?

Was it so hard?

Grunting at the confusion, Jimmelta stared at the bright, blue sky, which smiled on her small kingdom, and ate half a doughnut. There was nothing left to do in moments of anguish and despair, except have the other half. Distressed, she returned to the main worry on her mind, when her golden yacht could sail. She wanted to sail now. She thought her expertise tackling the sales in the Church of Harvey Nichols, was perfect preparation for the voyage ahead.

Where were all the floods? Was it so difficult to get one? Maybe a tycoon would do —or was it typhoon, or typhoo? Then she remembered that Typhoo was a brand of tea —and she couldn't imagine sailing in tea. Every other country had one, so why couldn't she? All she needed, in fact, was her own private flood: and, she didn't want to share it with anybody else.

She needed to get her amazing, iconic yacht into water, not stay stuck in the mud piles on the river bed. All this sunshine had to go, and it had to go now; otherwise she wouldn't be able to sail her handbag shaped yacht on holiday.

'If we can get men to the moon, why can't we make it rain?' growled Jimmelta showing her new pearly white gnashers.

She thought about her 'important' job, sharing pointless information on her chat show. Of course, most of all she thought about her ratings, as the chat show was one of the best. She thought how clever the public were to love it so much. Then pondered, about reports that the colour yellow would replace white. Or, whether charity really did begin at the Church of Harvey Nichols.

Again, she stared lovingly at her yacht, which was more than half the width of the river and sighed. The Cath Kidston embellished flowers on the sides had made such a difference –it really was unique, all hers.

From her golden tower she spotted the children playing on the deck of the ship. Polka pretending to be a pirate, and Gingham, steering, obviously playing the captain. The remaining two children brandished plastic swords in role as soldiers. In between all this, sailors tried to get the vessel moving, much to the amusement of the children. Paisley and Kidston after Cath scuttled across the deck fighting, disturbing the diligent sailors. Jimmelta was sure she saw the swordsmen cut something off one of them. She couldn't work out whether it was a hat or a head. Nonplussed, she licked her lips, savoured the grains of sugar, and thought about a doughnut – another one.

'What are you doing now?' questioned Piggers.

'Piggers! Isn't it beautiful? My own yacht! AND in gold. I love the flowers on the side – it's just so perfect,' Jimmelta trilled and quilled. 'Do you know, it was on national television? My "little, ordinary" boat, did you know? I didn't realise it could cause a national disaster – apparently there's a queue for other ships to get into the Thames. Well, they'll just have to wait. It's a shame we don't have two rivers, not just the Thames, river, then I could have my own.

'Piggers, are you listening? Can you do

something about the rain? Can you get a flood from somewhere? We need one, but make sure you get one with a bit of taste, rather exotic with a wonderful name.'

Piggers paused for a moment from his work––and he stared in horror at Jimmelta, as she clackered on in her conversation. She really was hopeless. Her general lack of understanding towards others was amazing and quite frightening.

'Is my yacht the biggest in the world?' she squinted into the gold tinted periscope for the hundredth time today.

'No, Doughy, I'm afraid not,' replied Piggers nervously. He had been dreading this moment.

'But you told me it was!' snarled Jimmelta, spinning round to face her husband, who prepared himself for her outcry. 'You said you'd checked all the sizes of the yachts in the whole world and MINE was the biggest and the best! What's happened? Is it a lot to ask for? I told you what I wanted!'

She stood facing him, her hands on her hips, her lips pursed together, covered in sugar and jam. 'So,' she said in a slow, booming voice, standing perfectly still, 'who dares to have a bigger, more beautiful yacht than mine?'

Looking down at his work, hiding behind his thick black rimmed glasses,Piggers whispered,'Some rich man in Russia called Oli Gark...'

'OLI WHO?' fumed Jimmelta,spitting out the name. 'And how do you know?'

'Well, umm, umm, he rang me up and asked for the dimensions...' whispered Piggers, now really quite frightened.

'What did he mention?' she bawled.

'No,no! The dimensions of the yacht!' he barked. 'Dimensions,' he continued in a 'mean how long and wide it is. And anyway, since the stupid thing has been stuck in the Thames for weeks, and has been on television, with the dimensions, I don't see the problem.'

He turned away from Jimmelta. But Jimmelta didn't understand and nor did she really care.

'It looks good, doesn't it, Piggers?' she purred as she nibbled a new raspberry doughnut. She caught the jam on her extending tongue, capable of scouring her lips, and the lower part of her face, for every ounce of jam - certainly not a pretty sight. Admittedly, when Jimmelta initially shared her yacht design to an array of ship builders, only one replied and gave a quote. The company, 'Pirate Pursuits Ltd', owned by the Short Jack Nickel family from Kurdistan, concocted all types of sailing vessels – at any cost! And boy, once they knew who Jimmelta was, they charged, sending countless bills for her to sign. In fact, Polka pointed out that, there were enough invoices to create a new type of wallpaper for Bullion Castle. (Polka's sharp wit was lost on Jimmelta. She failed to see the gravity of the comment, and replied it would be a shame to hide the gold walls, and didn't like the idea of the invoice wallpaper). Pirate Pursuits Ltd followed her every whim regarding the design, and allowed her to choose the materials for the yacht. No one in history, had designed and built a golden yacht, in the shape of a handbag.

'I don't know why there's so much fuss. Why can't we just knock out the road at the side of that large building? Then we would have so much more space to get it out to sea,' Jimmelta whimpered to Piggers, fed up hearing about the yacht. He'd promised his beautiful wife a boat, something to keep her happy and quiet. The design was terrible and he despaired of the trouble it caused each day in the Thames.

A knock on the tower door surprised them. Pinky Squat introduced an unexpected guest, who appeared stern, and spoke quietly.

'Sir, Mr Idiot?' The man nodded and passed Piggers a long, white, envelope, with a red wax mark on it. He stood back whilst it was opened. Piggers knew this was an important letter and he carefully prised the seal without breaking the red wax. He knew who it was from, but wasn't sure if it was going to be a positive message or not. Most letters from this particular person, tended to be a great honour, but this time, Piggers had doubts.

'Where are you from?' quizzed Jimmelta, as she scrutinized the tall, willowy man, with black hair, and a short black moustache. He was impeccably tidy, impeccably quiet and impeccably precise.

'This is a letter from Her Majesty regarding your...umm, yacht. She would like you to remove it from the Thames by the end of next week, so trading can resume up and down the river. She is quite upset and hopes you will agree to get it into deeper waters. Since you are neighbours, and have "popped" in, every now and then, for tea and...ummm, the "odd" doughnut,' he whispered, squinting his eyes. He turned away at the sight of Jimmelta as the last bit of a doughnut squeezed into her mouth, 'she hopes this will be fine. As neighbours, she hopes you will oblige.'

Piggers nodded in agreement and immediately said yes. His wife just stared at the royal messenger and then declared that for next Christmas, she wanted her one of her own, who came with a royal seal of approval.

'Well, we are trying our best,' responded Jimmelta, oblivious to the enormity of the demand. 'I mean, we've got the army, the navy, sailors, my servants, the builders and those special troops who do really dangerous things all trying to get it moving. The thing is: we need a flood. If we had one, it would just sail away and I could start my holiday.'

The tall, willowy man could not believe what he was hearing. There was no apology, no remorse, no guilt and no attempt to pay for all the agencies involved. Worse still, he was horrified that Jimmelta thought the weather could be controlled or bought –like a pair of wellies! NO, she really was too much. What the Queen demanded she always got, and she wanted this handbag shaped yacht out of 'her' Thames.

Quickly.

Very quickly.

'Well, why don't we just knock down a few buildings or dig out the sides of the Thames? Then I'm sure it would be all right...' continued Jimmelta, ignoring Piggers' attempts to keep his thoughtless wife quiet.

The royal messenger stood disgusted at the thought of historical buildings smashed to the ground, or ancient roads dug up for this terrible yacht. He could not think of anything worse than returning to the Queen and giving her such a dreadful message. Tears came to his eyes as he pictured Queen's kind face and her love for the ancestry and history of her land.

'No. No! We cannot deliver this message. I will inform the Royal Household that you are doing all you can to remove this this, this... thing from the Thames SOON.'

Unaware of the trouble she was causing, Jimmelta asked if he'd like to join her on her television show, The Daily Chew. He could meet some famous people. After refusing gracefully, the once calm and reserved Queen's messenger, ran for the door of the tower, opened it and fled, shouting, 'Noooooooo!'

What a strange man, mused Jimmelta, tugging at the belt on her waist and smiled. Her beloved yacht, was quite a feature for Londoners and tourists alike. She decided, perhaps it was the eighth wonder of the world, or just the main wonder of London. After all, everybody was probably bored of those old buildings, stuffy guards in those silly, frilly bloomers and knickers, that came down to their knees, who stood outside Buckingham Palace. How lucky the Londoners were to have something, so new and dazzling. Different from all the old stuff that lured tourists to the capital!

She looked down from the tower window and watched the the messenger disappear from sight. Staring at her yacht – Jimmelta decided there and then, it had to be moved into the waters, so she could start her holiday.

Chapter 2

At the bank of the Thames, frustrated soldiers, marines and members of the special forces jostled to shift the yacht. Jimmelta meandered through the crowds, towards the men, oblivious to the chaos surrounding her yacht.

'So, Commander, how is it all going?' she asked, turning towards a very tall, wide chested man, booming orders to men with shovels, and drills.

'Who are you? Can't you see the problem

this yacht is causing? London is grinding to a halt because nothing can move up and down the Thames. And gold! Who, in their right mind, would build a solid gold yacht...IN THE SHAPE OF A HANDBAG...WHO?'

Jimmelta, aware of the television cameras filming for news just nodded. Some how, she didn't think a glib comment was the best idea.

'Perhaps you should dig up the sides of the pavements. Or, maybe get some cranes and move it downstream to the sea. Or, just knock down a few unnecessary buildings,' she shouted above the noise of the equipment. The grey, smoky buildings, with large, rotting bricks were an eyesore to Jimmelta. Even the Houses of Parliament failed to impress Jimmelta on her list of attractions. Yes, London needed her golden yacht.

The commander stopped mid-sentence and glowered, as Jimmelta stuck up her nose, ready for an argument. Did she not understand the trouble this yacht was causing?

'Madam, I am sorry, I don't know who you are, but you obviously don't know very much about this yacht'

'I do. It's *mine*. And I designed it to copy *my* favourite handbag,' she replied firmly and very proudly. The commander threw his hands in the air, as he sniffed contemptuously, at this mismatched monstrosity, with a doughnut in her hand, and a tape measure around her bulging waist.

'Well, umm,umm, I have to say, madam, that this golden handbag is ruining trade in the Thames. Instead of sorting out a war abroad, I have to get this thing out!'

'Can't we just get it into one of these wharfs or something? I have to move it before Dotty's gives me a parking ticket and takes it off me. Come on! You have to think of something. Anyway, if you can get it out, I'll let you use it as part of the navy or marines– though, only where it's raining.'

Sighing at her generous offer, Jimmelta turned to the cameras, and gave her best smile for the viewers. Her brilliant idea, to design a yacht so big, was excellent for the ratings. The yacht made news everyday!

The commander, annoyed at her flippancy, decided the yacht, would, one way or another, be out of the Thames as soon as possible. Then London could get back to normal. So, his composure regained, he gently and politely told Jimmelta not to worry, and through gritted teeth, he wished her farewell.

As Jimmelta departed, reporters edged forward to ask details for tomorrow's show. Would she be inviting the commander once the yacht was at sea? Jimmelta merely smiled, waved and nodded to the hordes of crewmen. Then went inside Bullion Castle and up to the tower. Yes, she really suited the fame thing, and she smiled to herself.

Meanwhile, the children were anxious to start their holiday, and keen to sail somewhere other than the Thames.

'I think the boat's a bit too wide,' commented Gingham, climbing the golden mast and peering across to London Bridge through his periscope. He munched on a huge piece of chocolate cake, and pointed to several camera crews reporting on the yacht. 'That's the third one today, telling everyone on telly we're stuck.'

'Does that mean we're famous?' asked Paisley as he skidded on the floor past the soldiers. 'Does that mean I'll be on the television?' he queried, patting down his hair so the curls didn't stick out.

'Paisley, we're on television nearly every day because of the yacht, because it's too big to get out of the Thames,' replied Gingham, nonplussed, as tourists took photos of the Idiot spectacle. 'I think Mum made a big mistake when she drew the shape.'

While he spoke, workmen shaved off gold from parts of the yacht, and collected it into sacks. This really wasn't how they wished to spend their day, working for some silly television presenter.

Chapter 3

''ERE! Wha's tha' noise? Bangin' on the door at this time! Wha' time is it? It's meant to be my lie-in! DON' A SERVANT GET A BI' OF PEACE AN' QUIET ON A WEEK DAY? I'VE GOT A BUSY LIFE, AN' I AIN'T ANSWERING THE DOOR TILL LATER... SEE!' roared Rooster as the bells at Bullion Castle continued to ring.

'Aw, answer it, Rooster. Go on,' purred Pinky Squat from underneath his duvet covered with pictures of food. 'You know you're in charge.' With that, he turned on his side and went back to sleep, and snored so loudly, the curtains swayed.

'Why does it 'ave to be me who answers the door?' grumbled Rooster, as he put on a dressing gown. He made his way down the long corridor, and down the stairs to the enormous golden door. The boom of the bell deafened him. He hated this stupid thing, and thought it was noisy.

'Wha'd'ya want? It's six-thirty in the mornin' an' some of us 'ave a busy day ahead, so it betta be good!' Rooster snapped as he opened the door.

A tall, thin man in a suit, tie and bowler hat faced him. On both sides, he was flanked by men in uniforms with caps with plenty of badges and stripes, each looking pale, tired and serious.

'I am Sir Withamsplurt Trumplestumple-Smatchering-Splot, private secretary to the Queen and in charge of Her Majesty's armed forces. On my right is General Ditheringbody, and to my left is Wing Commander Hucklemuckle-Stigfast, both from the armed forces. Sir, we wish to speak to Jimmelta Chew van der Bratt...'

'She's asleep and don' get up till eleven before her show on this new boat of 'ers. Do you wanna make an appointment to see her?' Rooster asked, as he rubbed sleep out of his eyes. For the first time, he slowing absorbed the sight before him. These three men didn't look like flaky pop stars, reality contestants, or talent show hosts desperate to get a slot on Jimmelta's chat show and become famous for a day.

They didn't look like these sorts at all.

'Sir, I am here on behalf of the Queen. I am here to inform Jimmelta Chew van der Bratt that the armed forces, along with the ship builders, have got her ship, or yacht, or handbag FINALLY MOVING! It has taken the best part of two months to budge this monstrosity from our famous landmark, and in the process it has stopped countless boats and ship owners doing business. All in all, this, this, this is a stupid idea to have the worlds biggest yacht...'

'Handbag yacht, sir,' interrupted the wing commander, raising his eyes to the sky in distain.

"Yes, yes... a handbag shaped yacht. Well, whatever! The thing is, the yacht or bag or ship...is OUT OF THE THAMES AND IS NOW WAITING TO SAIL! Oh, and there's a bill from the armed forces for their work, one from the London Port Authorities and one from the Queen. Oh, and all the charities want to know what you're doing with the gold shavings. Good morning.' At that, the three men saluted Rooster, quickly turned on their heels and departed.

Tired, yawning and confused, Rooster took the bills and put them in the billing room. This was a vast, long room lined with golden desks, each piled high, with incoming and outgoing bills. All dealt with by the chief of bills later. Looking at the clock, Rooster decided it would be better if he could squeeze in another snooze before the family woke up to a breakfast cooked by Gingham. So Rooster rested on one of sofas and went back to sleep.

Banging and clashing woke him up once more

from a lovely dream. Piggers charged down the stairs, shouted he was late for a meeting.

'Rooster, I'm late!' he exclaimed. 'Why aren't you ready? What are you doing in a dressing gown, and shouldn't you be cleaning?'

Piggers couldn't understand all the changes since his return from Bolivia, where he had been held hostage by the Quintilla tribe. As Piggers questioned Rooster, Gingham popped his head from the kitchen to ask if anyone wanted breakfast.

'Look, Dad! I've made some chocolate fudge pancakes with cream and maple syrup! Hey, Rooster, d'you want one too? Dad! Come and have a taste!' Gingham was obviously delighted with his cooking. He wanted to share them with anyone who was awake –which happened to be Piggers and Rooster.

'Sorry, son, just off now and in a real rush. Oh, Gingham, make sure your mother gets that yacht moving today, now they've got it out of the Thames. And tell her WE'RE NOT TAKING A TELEVISION CREW ON HOLIDAY –ON THE YACHT...FOR THE FINAL TIME!'

Jimmelta's idea to host her chat show on the yacht wasn't popular with Piggers. Being filmed all the time, in between guests, wasn't his idea of fun. Piggers still wasn't sure about her new fame. This breakfast programme, The Daily Chew, was very popular with viewers. But all things considered, Piggers preferred the overweight, hopeless, rather selfish and unsure Jimmelta. This thinner, sharper, wittier, more confident wife, quite happy to have hamburgers with heads of state, was so different to the woman he'd married. She now fought to promote towels from the Church of Harvey Nichols to be delivered to prisons, in wrapped boxes smelling of floral perfume.

Piggers' life was different since Jimmelta's arrest for stealing doughnuts. Her time at Blackpool Illuminations, where she suffered at the mercy of Snailetta Bottom, seemed so far away. He remembered Reggie's list of cruel jobs which Jimmelata had to do each day. Worse, it was all televised as reality show. He wondered what became of those horrible people. He tried to imagine what they were doing now.

Reggie, he heard, was working in a dog meat factory and ground leftovers and scraps before boiling them in huge vats. The smell of roasted rats and entrails amused him! Snailetta was a litter collector for the M1 and M4 on Mondays, Wednesdays and Fridays. She worked between junctions, four to eight, in all types of weather. Her expensive and flamboyant clothes were replaced. She now wore a bright yellow, thick, plastic long coat with elasticated trousers, to stop the rain drench her underwear.

All concerned with Jimmelta's downfall were punished. The names of these horrible people were brandished on placards and adverts in cinemas throughout the country.

Piggers pondered about Jimmelta's new causes, especially the acquisition of Blackpool Illuminations. She renamed it 'The Pastel Pleasure Place' and resprayed the rides in her favourite pink and blue. Of course, the Church of Harvey Nichols was delighted to have the complete order for towels and scented soaps for the theme park causes.

The ratings for her chat show and ticket sales

for the theme park proved a success. And, she was his 'lovely wife' after all.

Now, he had to deal with her new mad idea. Her oddly, designed yacht, built in gold with so many problems. Although it was ready to sail, Piggers' instinct knew moving the yacht was beginning of their problems. He knew, the holiday would be far from plain sailing and predicted things wouldn't run to plan.

He knew how Jimmelta complicated things. Piggers braced himself for the holiday ahead, and knew something would go wrong!

Chapter 4

Leading up to the holiday, Jimmelta promised the children the trip of a lifetime. For Polka, Gingham and Paisley, this meant no school.

However, as a famous TV presenter there were problems, as she couldn't just take them out of school for a length of time. The current government made this sort of thing quite difficult. She needed to interview tutors who would educate and nurture her children, while they enjoyed the many splendid sights of

Marmalade Island. This island was the starting point of the holiday, near Ambergris Caye. It would be excellent for swimming, learning to dive and acclimatising to the heat. Jimmelta wondered whether, life had been easier when she was overweight, pretty useless, and clueless, on how to look after her children and educate them.

Everything was different now. She knew nearly all the letters of the alphabet, and was confident at reading words with more than two or three syllables. She felt her newly accomplished intelligence worthy of hiring the best tutors money could buy. And, she certainly intended to do just that. While the company built the yacht, Jimmelta organized the task of hiring a tutor. She asked the Inherited Australian Convicts to help sift through the application forms. She explained to them the importance of one. They couldn't understand it at all.

'I ain't gettin' it. Why do they need a tutor when there's three of us?' questioned Pinky Squat. 'We can do a bi' of maths an' stuff an' get some 'istory goin' about places. Yeah! I reckon we'd 'ave some fun...' he added, as he picked up clothes strewn on the floor. Jimelta listened to the comments and ideas from Pinky Squat as she prepared for her show.

'Well, Pinky, under normal circumstances I'd say your plan to teach the children yourselves would be brilliant, but...' She paused, quite surprised at her sharpness of mind, and then said, 'I have a public duty as the presenter of The Daily Chew not to give my children a poor education.'

'We ain't poor!' shouted Pinky Squat. 'We sailed from Australia in a boat and passed loads of countries an'stuff!'

'I know, Pinky! And we think that's great. But since I'm on television every day, I have to have a proper tutor. You can all help out, and fill in with things the tutor can't do – like, err, rowing, building a fire, keeping the sides of the yacht spanking clean, crisp and golden. Anyway, you'll all have fun deciding who I should interview.'

Suddenly, she spun around and said, 'I think I am going to open the hunt for a tutor up to my public! What a brilliant idea! What d'you think?' she asked in a profound voice - the one she kept for reading school reports.

The three men glanced at each other and smiled. They knew Jimmelta, and the process would be filled with problems. They envisaged terrible things happening, with the nation transfixed on the competition… just like them!

'Yes! I'll say something this morning on The Daily Chew and tell anybody interested to contact one of you three…' Using her fingers to count out the Inherited Australian Convicts, Jimmelta checked there were three – she needed to get it right for the show.

'Fing is, what do we do if we can't read wha' they say?' pondered One-Eared Lumpy, now a little worried about the huge pressure on his flabby shoulders.

'Oh.' Jimmelta smiled, and gazed at herself in a golden mirror, with polka dot Cath Kidston bows surrounding it. 'We'll just pick out the words we can read, or ones that sound exciting. Or, we could get Piggers, oh and Gingham, to look at them. Gingham's quite good at this sort of thing. His teachers say he's good at picking out key words. He's good at something called "cloze procedure". Though, I don't understand that, because there's nothing in the Church of Harvey Nichols about it. They do have a dressing service, though.'

How important and intelligent Jimmelta felt, deciding the process of picking the right tutor. Not for her an agency. Not for her a discreet appointment. No, her children's education would be public property, viewers voting for their choice!

She thought how clever she was. How brilliant she was. And, how astute to involve the public in her children's education! How exciting! Imagine a tutor picked by the viewers! How new.

How wonderful.

Jimmelta wondered if her idea was bit like a lottery. She'd never thought of education like this before. She then asked the Inherited Australian Convicts to make a list of skills necessary, to educate her precious offspring. All looked blank.

'A list?' choked Rooster, who started to panic – the thought of writing and making notes and readin' stuff worried him. He wasn't familiar with these skills at all.

'Is there a problem?' Jimmelta purred, as she tried on a new, summer garden hat, (which resembled a tractor). 'I thought you'd all love to be involved. There! Do you like my new designer hat, especially for the garden party at Buckingham Palace? Dotty said to do something unusual. So I went to her hatter maker, or whatever they're called, and asked for a special, unique (that's a new word I've learnt) hat. I said, I wanted to stand out from the crowd. They said this would certainly do the trick! So what do you think?'

She pouted and posed in front of the mirror, and thought how wonderful she looked. The Inherited Australian Convicts gasped in horror. From the back of the hat, where the silk and straw-like tractor was placed, they saw a trickle of oil dropping onto her clothes! Jimmelta smiled.

'Isn't it marvellous? They said, the oil was a special touch. And, nobody, not even Dotty, or any of her tribe, would have anything quite like this. They called it a masterpiece.' She smirked and bent down to wipe the oil on the golden floor, with a specially designed rag, which coordinated with the hat. It was so different, so clever, and so terribly expensive. She put the hat away to keep it safe and clean until the garden party the following day.

Chapter 5

The next day, late morning, Jimmelta dressed for the special occasion. She heaved herself into her dress and anchored it down with safety pins so it wouldn't blow up in the wind. She didn't want to show her triple layered underwear, which sucked in her bottom and the tops of her legs. Fastening her tractor hat down with wood and ceramic glue, she made sure it was firmly stuck in place. She wanted her hat to be the most admired at the garden party.

The royal garden party was the social event of the year, with many people invited to Buckingham Palace, to be thanked for their hard work and services to their country. Hundreds of tourists flocked to the gates of the palace. The guests proudly entered through the side gate, showing their beautifully inscribed invitations to the guardsman and attendants. Some arrived on foot, others by taxi, some, like Piggers and Jimmelta, by personalised limousine. The queues were orderly and very happy, as it was an honour to be invited. Neither Idiot had been awarded a medal, or done anything worthwhile in the community. However, Jimmelta was very popular with the public, and was able to sway opinion to suit her programme.

Initially, as she glided out of the golden car and walked in front of Piggers, the crowds cheered.

But suddenly they stopped in amazement. They saw the monstrosity on her head, and the black drips at the nape of her neck. She waved and smiled, the lights from reporters' cameras flashed furiously without stopping. Jimmelta grinned once more. She knew her hat was a sensation.

It certainly was.

But maybe not in the way she had anticipated. In the meantime, the excited guests weaved through the paths leading to the gardens. Here, numerous tents were bursting with cakes, sandwiches, champagne, tea, coffee, and many more afternoon tea delights.

Aeroplanes flew in patterns above, as entertainment for the party. Crowds everywhere gasped, cheered and clapped at the aerobatic stunts filling the sky.

The Queen handed out hundreds of honours and medals for a wealth of lifetime commitments. These ranged from knighthoods, to important letters after names. The Queen, elegant, charming and courteous, acknowledged the Idiots and spoke to them about the weather. Jimmelta, unable to contain her pride, at using the Queen's personal milliner, discussed her own hat and its unique appeal. A distant look of horror passed across the royal eyes as Jimmelta proceeded to show the designer oil from the back of the hat. It dripped in designer splats onto her expensive dress.

As the Queen carefully, and seamlessly removed herself from the embarrassing spectacle, the nearby crowd stared at the catastrophe on top of Jimmelta's head.

'Is she mad?' asked a gentleman who had just

been knighted as Sir Wintrup de Saltsneese. He wiped his glasses and spoke to his wife. The wife replied, she had no doubt, anyone who attended a royal garden reception, wearing a tractor on top of her head, as a hat, was definitely not mad, but completely mad.

'D'you know,' whispered Jimmelta to Piggers, as the Queen shook hands with guests, 'I think she was jealous of my hat. Don't you think I'm right, Piggers?' she asked. She frowned at her husband, who almost fainted in disgust at the thought.

Piggers answered, as if the Queen was his own flesh and blood. 'The Queen never gets jealous, and has no need to!' Jimmelta turned away, only to be greeted by a host of laughing garden guests all pointing at her amazing hat.

'Well,' she shouted to the hordes of people,

'at least I have been brave enough to try a new design, even if it's slightly out of place! Isn't this how great statements are made? Isn't this how new ideas develop? Shame on you all for making fun of my hat!' And with that she pushed her way through the crowd to the edge of the garden and sat down on a bench.

'Actually, I think it's great,' said the voice of someone towering over Jimmelta. She cried and felt humiliated by all those wonderful people. She was ashamed, and looked down at the perfectly manicured grass, and she sniffled. As the designer oil dripped down the nape of her neck, Jimmelta stared at the shiniest, black, pointed shoes she had ever seen. The shoes were laced, very tightly, and were on a pair of very long feet. The bottoms of the grey striped trousers met the glistening shoes.

'I said, I think your hat's rather great amongst all those stuffy hats whose wearers are trying to impress her. She's not, you know. She sees millions of exclusive hats on women every day. Now this, well, my dear, this is quite something else. I particularly like the oil at the back of the tractor, very, very realistic. Well done, my dear, I am cheered enough now for the day.'

'Well, I must be off and get my sword sorted out for these knighthoods. They take ages. Of course, we've tried to pare down the ceremony, but everyone wants their bit to go on and on and on – I can't tell you how long it takes. But this hat, well, as mad as it is, it matches that handbag! I found the whole thing amusing...'

And as Jimmelta finally finished blowing her nose and wiping her eyes, the booming voice disappeared amongst the crowds. Jimmelta convinced the speaker was a very important person – said thank you. Though she wasn't quite sure who he was. The day continued in much the same fashion, as swathes of guests gasped at her hat. After the stranger praised Jimmelta's individual attire, she felt proud discussing the significance of her rural headgear.

Piggers, knew this was just one of Jimmelta's daily horrors, and chatted happily with an ordinary couple. They talked about the extraordinary things they'd done in their community. They were quiet, charming, unassuming and content with the simple things in life.

The sound of Jimmelta yelling broke the polite conversations. A tall, skinny woman with a rather big nose shouted at Jimmelta. The woman made a funny comment regarding hat.

In response, Jimmelta took an umbrella nearby and stuck it in the black hat with the red feather. A scuffle broke out, and Jimmelta threw the tractor from her hat at the tall, skinny woman, who cried.

Once again, the crowds stared at Jimmelta. Her hair looked like a haystack from the tractor, her lipstick was smeared, her tights were holed and laddered. The heels of her high shoes now prodded her opponent. Piggers hung his head, he didn't know what to do.

'Come here, Jimmelta. This simply isn't good enough at the royal garden party, you should know better. Especially since we're neighbours! Come here and tidy yourself up. What will people think? And you'd better make sure this doesn't leak out to the press! They'll have a field day...'

As Piggers finished his sentence, two plain clothed detectives whisked her away.

'Piggers!' yelled Jimmelta at the top of her voice, 'save me from the Queen's police! Quick, they're taking me to the dungeons and they might chop off my head! HELP ME!' she screamed as she tried to wriggle her way out of their grip.

'Oi, madam, may I say...' shouted a man in a top hat as she passed by, 'I doubt if they'll execute you, but they should certainly do something about that ridiculous hat!' Roars of laughter followed the comment.

In the tent the detectives pulled up a chair, plonked her on it. They then questioned her. They realised that Jimmelta wasn't just a security hazard – but she was a hazard, full stop.

'So, madam, it's a little disappointing. You've

let the royal garden party down and ended up in a brawl,' the first detective said. Jimmelta looked on blankly. This episode would either be amazing for her ratings or terrible. She recalled the terrible incident over the stolen doughnuts, the judge and the Blackpool Illuminations – it was all so humiliating, especially having to clean out stalls on television. A shudder ran down her spine at the memories of Reggie and Snailetta Bottom. She gulped and cried:

'Everybody laughed at my hat, made by the Queen's hatter! I said I wanted to be different, and I ended up looking foolish. And I paid a lot of money to look like thissssssssssss.' And Jimmelta howled.

'May I say madam, you really didn't have to spend so much money to look this stupid – you could have done it for nothing,' said the smaller, balder detective of the two.

After a nail biting time for Jimmelta, both detectives nodded to each other, yawned, then smirked.

'Madam, you're free to go back to the party and reclaim your magnificent hat.'

So meekly, red eyed and still sniffling, Jimmelta nodded, said thank you and left the tent. As she walked away, she heard roars of laughter from inside. However, this was muffled by the brass band and low flying aeroplanes. Finally, she found Piggers soaking up the summer sun and drinking tea.

'Oh, Piggers, it was so awful in tent. They made fun of me, those policemen or detectives, whatever they're called. I didn't know the hat would look so stupid! I thought having Dotty's hat maker would be a wonderful thing. Now I look so silly,' she cried.

Piggers leant forward put his arms around his crumpled wife and patted her hair and bits of the tractor. He hoped the press would have mercy on her.

'There there, Doughy, these things happen. It's not quite the end of everything. I thought the hat was rather funny – besides, you have to set a trend,' he whispered. She blew her nose, wiped her eyes on a spare tissue. He didn't mind; he quite liked it when she appeared hopeless. It reminded him of how she used to be before the doughnuts, jail and Blackpool Illuminations.

Jimmelta pulled out the remaining parts of her hat and tidied her hair. She dabbed her eyes and smiled sweetly, then whispered, 'I must apologise for being so upset with the tall, thin lady,' and she left Piggers to find her victim.

The tall, skinny lady, with the big nose, and black pointed hat, still regaled guests, with the details of the umbrella attack. She obviously exaggerated wherever possible, to make Jimmelta appear like a monster. She edged through the crowd, and Jimmelta faced her victim.

'Madam, from the bottom of my heart, I would like to apologise for being so terrible. My hat, has caused nothing but laughter and mockery today, even though it was made by the Queen's hatter. Though it saddens me, I accept it was a source of amusement. Do accept my apology.'

With this said, Jimmelta her out her hand to shake it. The startled lady, laughed and flung her arms around Jimmelta. The guests clapped and cheered, as Jimmelta smiled. Suddenly the hat didn't seem so important – having fun was much, much nicer.

Jimmelta and Radishetta Trupplepump laughed, walked arm in arm and enjoyed the day very much. Piggers looked on from afar at the scene and smiled. Jimmelta seemed so happy. Then he noticed the back of her dress covered in black oil from the tractor hat. He raised his eyes to the sky and hoped she wouldn't discover it until she got back to Bullion Castle.

Then, a familiar shriek caught her husband's attention. Piggers turned and chatted to another very nice couple, and pretended to ignore the sounds of tears and laughter. Nearby, a man in black shoes and pin striped trousers smirked at the shrieks. He then handed the Queen another list of names. He put his sword into its sheath, whilst a corgi bit at his heels and entertained the crowds. Being royal, he thought, was funnier some days than others.

And so the day ended well. Back home, Jimmelta and Piggers had a cup of tea. They entertained the children with stories about the tractor hat with designer oil.

Chapter 6

The search for the tutor began once the yacht's construction commenced. Jimmelta announced to the nation a competition to find the perfect tutor for her sweet, endearing children. She struggled with the details and said her producer would send out a list of requirements to anyone who was interested. By the time she finished, the switch board was jammed with viewers wishing to get application forms for the tutor job.

Stout-nosed and pointy-nosed. They came with hair, without hair, with spots, without spots, in clean clothes, in starched clothes, looking flea-infested, in smelly clothes, in mouldy clothes, with smelly socks, without smelly socks, snot-infested, clean-nailed, grubby-nailed and no-nailed. They were with teeth, without teeth, with fillings, without fillings, with twitches, without twitches, with limps, without limps, and some, with gargling belches. They came with tattoos, without tattoos, with music blaring out loud, with speakers and without speakers. They came, each one unsuitable in the eyes of the children.

Dotty wanted Jimmelta to begin this adventure and sail away from her beloved wharfs and the Thames. Then life could resume as normal –life before the golden handbag.

They were in a rush.

They had no tutor… and time was running out. A tutor was needed.

Since the request on her show for a tutor, the applications kept on arriving. Candidates kept arriving at the door of Bullion Castle. All from every part of the globe, each sure they had that special quality to enthuse and engage the children with their studies. Most candidates wanted to be famous, and each was sure, working with the children improved their chances. In truth, Jimmelta didn't really know what qualities she was looking for in a tutor, and she certainly didn't know how to read the countless letters of application for the job. Norris, the bleary eyed producer, whose job it was to trawl through each, was now twitching from working so hard. He was constantly confused by Jimmelata's views and decisions, so no longer asked for her opinion. His flustering and nervousness had given way to impatience and urgency – to find a tutor.

Everything suddenly made sense to Norris Quipperley-Sikes. He realised his boss found reading long words, with letters that 'went up to the sky,' very confusing. He discovered, certain blends made her pronounce words with a stutter and a stumble. 'Ph' words soon became 'the f's without a f' and 'Cy' became 'that s'. Norris watched Jimmelta scour letters for short land lying words, such as 'want' and 'sun' and 'news'. She said the little letters were much more important than the long ones, or the droopy ones.

So Norris, bright as an academic button on a Cambridge shirt, and sharp as the scientific ray of a postgraduate razor, ignored her. He felt it was his duty to find the children someone who could change their world and broaden their horizons. Yes, Norris had put himself in charge of the situation, and he would soon inform the press of their choice. It was his mission to find a tutor who would organise the children's lives and do this strange thing: educate them. He needed someone to challenge and prepare them for future life.

And indeed she would.

She arrived at the castle with a large, brown, battered,suitcase held together by a leather belt. Only the back of her frame could be seen as she faced the huge door of Bullion Castle to ring the bell. Her frizzy, curly hair was sort of darkish, with red streaks plonked amongst it to add colour or personality – or, to compensate for the terrible haircut. She was quite small, so that the suitcase was nearly half her height, and she clasped the handle as if she was guarding a fortune. A black overcoat covered her clothes. From beneath the hemline and above the flat, black shoes, stripy tights were visible, in bright yellow, green and red, encasing rather wide legs. 'I AM HERE FOR THE JOB AS

TUTOR TO THOSE SPOILT CHILDREN,'
she bellowed when Rooster opened the door.

Rooster stood speechless at the vision front of him. So far, the candidates had been eccentric, slightly different, but nobody had been strong, dominant or loud. Rooster looked at this tough, determined woman – small and round, like a sumo wrestler – who was definitely not going to be ignored or teased.

'Umm, who did you say you were?' he asked as he eyed up the tough-looking stranger.

'I didn't,' she boomed sounding like a muffled drill. 'I saw the advert and thought I'd come to see the children to decide whether I could stomach them.'

He listened, this was the only candidate to declare whether she wanted the job, and could tolerate the children. The potential tutors interviewed by Norris and the Inherited Australian Convicts had all, without exception, expressed their love of the children and their desire to educationally enrich their lives.

This was a first.

Rooster didn't like the sound of her gravelly, booming voice with its odd squeak. He saw a tough, maybe horrid tutor. In fact, Rooster wondered if she liked children. He wasn't impressed at all. 'So, umm, umm, just before I get the family up out of bed...' he started, only to be interrupted.

'It's six-thirty,and they're ALL STILL

in BEDDDDDDD?' Her voice sounded like the clashes of thunder, ready to strangle everything in its path. The lights shook, the curtains moved as she blew the heat of her breath around. The ancestral paintings along the corridors slid from their hinges; there wasn't a perfectly hung painting in sight.

'Well, umm, it's busy work finding a tutor. And the little children have been involved as well. In their own way,' replied Rooster, who wished he'd stayed in bed and ignored the doorbell.

Too late.

'Well, I AM HERE! GET THEM UP AT ONCE!' she bellowed. She stormed into the golden dining room, slung her old suitcase against the golden walls. Then she slumped onto a golden chair and waited with her arms folded.

'GET THEM UP NOW!'

Rooster scurried off up the golden stairs, pulling his nightshirt from under his feet so he didn't slip, and ran as fast as he could to Jimmelta's room. He shook with fear and excitement at the prospect of having her as the tutor. He wiped his brow, straightened his dressing gown and knocked on the bedroom door. Jimmelta was a heavy sleeper, and it took time to answer. Finally, bleary eyed, she opened the door. Her hair was in huge golden rollers, a face pack plastered over her divine skin, a frilly, long dressing gown wrapped around her and a telescope was clasped in her left hand.

'What is it, Rooster? It's only somewhere around six or seven…What is it? You look white. Why are you shaking?' quizzed a tired but curious Jimmelta. She didn't like to be disturbed when gawking at her wonderful yacht through her telescope.

'She's here…' he said, jumbling his words, 'you know, she's… it's… her…she's here'

'What are you rambling on about? You sound like someone who can't match their clothes! I have very important things to do. I need to get ready to inform the nation about worldly matters, such as, where to get golden sails for your yacht and, if rubies are really the new diamond! I have a busy day!' Jimmelta retorted to the unusually quiet Rooster.

He beckoned her to the top of the stairs, not daring to say a word. Jimmelta followed. She always liked a little adventure.

Below they heard the pounding of footsteps, a bit like a localised earthquake without any of the fallout.

Quietly, Jimmelta whispered to Rooster, 'What is that noise? Have we got a burglar? Who is it?' she quizzed, turning to him.

'It's her. She said she's…the new tutor…'
'What! We haven't decided yet!' gasped Jimmelta in amazement.

'No, we're not deciding, she is. Just see her. You'll know what I mean,' Rooster answered, sheepishly pointing downstairs.

Gingerly, feeling rather scared, Jimmelta crept silently down to the hall. Peeking around the golden door of the dining hall, she gasped in horror and complete disbelief. This thing… woman…tutor…somebody to teach her children looked as if she had not changed for a week, or maybe a month. Worse, her shoes were worn. But even worse, far worse, she smelt of fields and things, and she wasn't wearing any lipstick!

'So just who are you? I am not expecting any visitors,' shouted Jimmelta at the small, fat woman with pursed lips and hands on her hips, who looked decidedly angry at having waited so long for a response.

'WELL, YOU'RE LATE COMING DOWN, AREN'T YOU?' stated the woman, glancing around the room with an air of disgust. 'I'M NOT SURE I WISH TO

TUTOR SUCH A LAZY AND TASTELESS LOT,' she continued to march up and down the room. She snorted and turned her nose up at the golden décor and furnishings. As she moved everything, including Jimmelta and Rooster, shook.

Once again Rooster, now joined by Pinky Squat and One-Eared Lumpy, asked who she was. The other two Inherited Australian Convicts looked on very glum. The whirls of frizzy dark hair, with dyed streaks nestled like blobs of wild velcro stuck onto her forehead. By her ears the hair stuck out with nowhere to go.

'THE NAME'S ANCLAVIA NEFEETA REFEETA-OTURIA-LAPSPRIG,' she announced in a voice that swirled and swished, deeply through the Bullion household.

'That's a big name,' answered Jimmelta, horrified by her appearance. Then, to sound powerful, she asked, 'Does that mean you have lots of letters in it?' She stroked her golden curlers, checking her bouncing hair.

'Well, I can see I'm certainly needed here,' continued Anclavia Nefeeta Refeeta-Oturia- Lapsprig, 'so when shall I start?'

They all stood speechless, motionless, and looked hopeless – it had been decided; or rather, she had decided.

Miss Refeeta-Oturia-Lapsprig pounded the floors of the dining room, openly displaying her contempt for the golden furniture, golden walls and golden framed pictures hanging on the wall. She snorted so loudly the table and chairs shook.

The Inherited Australian Convicts looked on. Jimmelta couldn't imagine the response from the children. She looked on with sadness, knowing they would have to work. She wanted to ask this imposing, monstrous woman to leave. But Jimmelta stood quiet. Then Anclavia Nefeeta Refeeta-Oturia-Lapsprig swung towards her and demanded the children get up. The servants meekly shuffled away to get them, whilst Jimmelta decided Piggers needed to deal with the monstrosity.

Chapter 7

One yacht later, and one tutor later, the Jimmi Chew was ready to leave the wharf.

After months of inconvenience in the Thames the Jimmi Chew was ready to sail. Except it kept getting stuck. At Bullion Castle the Inherited Australian Convicts frantically packed suitcases, supplies of food, water bottles, household equipment and toys for the children. The children, in turn, packed books, pens, pencils, everything they needed for their tutorials.

The tutor was determined to make these spoilt rascals have more backbone. She sincerely hoped there would be one or two struggles for them to overcome. Smirking, with her arms folded, she watched as Gingham, Polka and Paisley gathered their belongings, and then checked nothing had been overlooked. Even Jimmelta felt sorry for her children. They would now have to work with this enormous lump, this wrestler of a tutor, and it sent a shudder through her body.

'I can't believe our brilliant adventure as modern day pirates is going to be ruined by her,' snarled Paisley. He glowered with fury, his adventure ruined with school work. He still blazed with rage with his father's decision.

He knew he was going to hate the holiday now – not even his mother's chat show could entertain him. He shuddered. Everything was going to be awful. School was a better choice now!

'Me too, I agree' replied Polka secretly determined not to do more work than necessary. The servants shuffled, gathering the luggage together to be delivered to the yacht.

'Cor, half of me wishes we didn' have to go. I don' fink I'll get on with her,' said Pinky Squat, looking at the monstrous hulk overseeing the children's every move. 'I jus' can't imagine wha' it's gonna be like with her on board. Poor ol' Jimmelta. She will 'ate it.'

'Well, boys, it ain't as if they're roughin' it, are they?' replied Rooster.

'Maybe we'll ask to stay here an' sort things out. We don' need to be on the yacht, do we? Besides, we've got loads to do with all them animals an' stuff, an' we do deserve a break too!' butted in One-Eared Lumpy. No, they had to go with the family, like it or not.

While they discussed the children, Jimmelta panicked. She was having a cacophony of disasters —nothing quite in the same league as the tractor hat, but to her mind, not far behind. Her outfits for interviews on the yacht needed to be sorted.

Normally, a wardrobe mistress chose one each day. Her favourite clothes were outrageous, and more fitting for a fancy dress party, making her look quite ridiculous.

More importantly, she worried about her doughnut craving, and a huge supply to satisfy her hunger on the adventure. So she ordered hundreds of boxes to be dropped onto the yacht. After many visits to the yacht with endless supplies, the family was finally ready to depart into the great unknown.

Well- sort of!

Finally boarding the most famous, or infamous, of yachts, Jimmelta shed a tear or two, but decided three tears was far too generous.

Piggers quietly disappeared below deck, the rest of the family waved to the crowds from the deck, jumping with joy. This was short lived, as their tutor insisted they did press-ups in public to develop their strength! Jimmelta walked to the other end of the deck and continued waving to her public.

Getting the yacht into safer waters was riveting, industrial cranes eased it down the Thames without knocking down any landmarks. Crowds watched in awe. The metal giants, on the command of generals from the armed forces, pushed the golden monstrosity and guided it out towards the water.

'Isn't she beautiful?' sighed Jimmelta, wiping a tear from her eyes as she waved her 'little' boat to its new home. She turned towards the cameras, and added, 'I am just so thrilled the people, my people, enjoyed the yacht each day in the Thames. Naturally, it's been wonderful to have so many guests on board, especially all those men in uniforms…' she smiled.

Above the throngs of exuberance, set back from the crowd, standing on very high scaffolding, the Queen, jumped and laughed for joy. The golden 'splurge' disappeared down the Thames. At either side of the Jimmi Chew's enormous frame, the generals laughed, and threw their hats into the air, clapping and dancing. Jimmelta felt honoured. If only she realised they were all just so glad to get rid of her silly yacht.

She felt even more important than the royal family. And dreaming again of future fortunes, she imagined being over at Dotty's place, Buckingham Palace, eating a doughnut or two, wearing a crown and playing with corgis, and regaling all with her exploits. She wondered if this was what it felt like to be the most important person in England. Fancy, the Queen, taking time out from her busy schedule, to come and wave the family off! She knew she was a 'secret royal best friend' or a, SRBF! The yacht sailed past the landmarks ready to greet the sea. Jimmelta felt just like an explorer beginning a great voyage. She wondered what her family would bring back from their journey. Obviously, potatoes and chocolate were out. Maybe a new face cream, or a musical lipstick. How thrilling to become an explorer.

She clutched the notes, (all in four or five letter words,) for her first chat show on the yacht, and wore a gold threaded life jacket embellished with pink, orange and purple f lowers. Then Jimmelta spoke with great pride to her beloved viewers:

'Well, here we are on my very own Jimmi Chew, even bigger than my feet' – she sniggered. – 'Waved off by my adoring fans and devoted Dotty! We're off to the shores where new and exciting adventures take place, with many people to interview. Dear viewers, how lucky you are to share my adventures.' Then, as she stumbled across a longer word, her conversation trailed off.

By the time it had reached the estuary, she felt like an explorer ready to conquer the earth. By the time she was in open water, with the shore behind, she wondered and wondered. By the time she was in the Channel, as far as she could see, there was only sea and the odd small boat. Suddenly, the largest, or nearly largest, yacht in the world seemed small in this blanket of blue sea.

Everything seemed so small. Everything seemed so quiet.

Everything seemed so odd: no roads, no shops, no buildings, no traffic lights, no designer hats, sandwiches or cars - and, not a strand or smidgen of the Church of Harvey Nichols in sight.

Just sea, and lots of it.

Of course, the children were thrilled to be away from home, cut off from the rest of the world, except the crew for the chat show – and the tutor. The tutor, what a horrific thought. Jimmelta blotted the picture out of her mind, as the worry might ruin her hair – and that could never happen.

She surveyed the ocean. So this was what it felt like, being at sea, and this was what it looked like. Now, impatient to reach their island and not be too long at sea, she stood on the deck, waiting for hours, expecting Marmalade Island to appear- but it didn't. It was further away than she thought- much further away. Her joy of being on the handbag shaped yacht was short lived.

Jimmelta suddenly realised her adventure in warmer climes, on a new exciting island, meant enduring weeks at sea. With nothing but the English Channel and Atlantic Ocean wasn't something she, or the children relished, even during the summer. Jimmelta was bored, 'Piggers,' do you think we should get the Jimmi Chew to our island, then we could f ly out to join it? It's going to be so dull just on the sea without anything to do, except my show and working with that, that thing – the tutor.' Jimmelta waited for Piggers to respond.

'Well, in theory that could be a good idea,' he said. 'But somehow, I think the long days at sea will be perfect for the children. And I think the new tutor will get the children working.'

Jimmelta listened to his answer. This meant days at sea without any land in sight! There was only one thing to do and that was to cry, as she normally did. But no amount of wailing and blubbering would change Piggers' mind.

Now she was at sea, Jimmelta couldn't see what was so special to see about the sea. Still not convinced that sailing across the Atlantic was in the least bit interesting or worthwhile, she decided to ignore Piggers' common sense. She contacted the navy, and asked if it was possible to 'push' the yacht towards a really hot island, even if it meant, forgetting about their duty. Quick as a f lash, the answer from the other end of the phone was positive and perfect: they were only too happy to help their wonderful national treasure.

Thrilled with the result, Jimmelta told Piggers of the new decision. She smiled – how perfect the adventure was going to be, once they'd found Marmalade Island with the wonderful beach and sea. And, thank goodness for the help from the armed forces. Jimmelta was so grateful, and she knew her children would be too.

Chapter 8

Once the yacht finally sailed to her island, and moored in the bay the family boarded their flight to start their holiday. The plane circled the tiny island, the sun shone in the bright blue sky and the brilliant turquoise waves gently bobbed to the shore, and covered the white sand as the tide trickled in. She scanned the coastline below, and smiled. The yacht was already moored.

It was all perfect.

From the back of the aircraft she heard the tutor bellow at the children. They had to write in their diaries, their first impressions of the island. Polka, engrossed by the sight of such a magical place, ignored the 'The Tank', as they now called her. (Obviously, this was done out of earshot).

'Piggers, did we buy this island? Is it ours, or does it belong to this country?' asked Jimmelta, peering out of the window. She watched the palm trees sway in the breeze.

Piggers had a worried expression on his face. Surely she didn't want him to buy this as well! Deciding not to answer, he ignored the question. 'Can you see my yacht? Can you see the Jimmi Chew? Where is it?'

Jimmelta asked anxiously, disappointed it wasn't towering above the tiny, idyllic island in the middle of nowhere. As the plane circled over the green, luscious mountains, the golden handbag shaped mast sparkled in the distance. She smiled and purred. Her 'little' yacht was so magnificent, sort of like, a new Statue of Liberty, which meant freedom to the American people. This, in her eyes, reflected greatness, and of course, excitement. The expanse of gold shone in the sunlight, every angle, line and contour glistened, casting shards of light and reflections across the water. It was so big, so wide, so long, it looked like a small island...golden, of course. Squinting, she recognised the beautifully embellished flowers, on each side of the yacht in blues, pinks, (lots of pinks), and green. Her yacht was a dazzling expanse, majestic and powerful, and dominated the shore. She felt like a conquering queen. This thought was disturbed by the loud deafening voice of her 'favourite person' The Tank.

'WELL! HAVE YOU WRITTEN ABOUT YOUR PLANE JOURNEY?' she boomed to the bleary eyed children, who truly despised their new, enthusiastic tutor. Kidston after Cath still slept contentedly. Once again she asked them about their work. No one replied.

Then Gingham shuffled in his seat, tears of hatred in his eyes, and thrust a piece of work into her huge, hairy, clump-like hands.

Breaking away from her doodles and

designs, Polka handed her work in without a word and turned away. Not only did she dislike the military strictness of The Tank, she had really bad body odour. When she raised her arms, a waft of mouldy cheese and sweaty socks, stenched the immediate area. Jimmelta looked on, bemused, at the spectacle. How strange, she thought. Then she wondered if they knew all the letters of the alphabet and could write words with more than four or five letters. She studied The Tank, who resembled a small, menacing, smelly squat who boomed and squeaked, like a mixture of a tornado and a strangled animal. Jimmelta held her nose with a golden scented nose peg. Another wave of smelly cheese and sweaty socks attacked her delicate nostrils. She decided at the earliest opportunity, to push the tutor overboard – for a wash. Perhaps, she might be eaten by fish, whales, or even, a shark. What a wonderful thought, sighed Jimmelta. The Inherited Australian Convicts observed how she treated the children – and they also didn't like it.

'Fing is, Rooster, I know them children can be a bi' spoil' an' all, but they ain't baddddd,' commented One-Eared Lumpy, Rooster and Pinky Squat nodded.

'We ain't gonna get 'er on our side neither. She don't like us 'cos we don' write much. I said how we 'ad changed fings an' she was havin' none of it,' added Pinky Squat. Peering out of the cabin window, he smiled at the beautiful weather. A scowl followed when he heard orders blasted to the children about their belongings.

Jimmelta quietly decided The Tank had to go. She had a cruel streak. She knew, scented towels and fragrant soaps, from the Church of Harvey Nichols would be wasted on this person. The camera crew filmed the family on arrival. This indicated the start of live chat shows from the yacht.

Jimmelata appeared onto the steps of the plane and smiled. As the first member of the family, she stood and surveyed the scene in front.

One by one the children trundled down the steps to the sandy ground and roared with with joy at the wonderful location.

Paisley and Gingham threw their arms in the air and jumped up and down. They even forgot about The Tank, who oozed her way down steps, grimacing. Jimmelta kissed her children in delight, whilst Piggers smiled at the beauty of the island.

Chanting from behind the trees, interrupted the quiet scene. All too quickly, Jimmelta, her children and the chaotic crew, oh, – and The Tank –were greeted by islanders. They wore hats, danced, and made weird music made from branches of trees and fruit.

'Cor, look!' Paisley pointed, as one of them, presented the family with fruit in a rattan bowl. 'Cor, we have our own dancers coming to say hello!' He waved to the natives.

The rest grinned, whilst Jimmelta rushed forward to shake their hands. The main dancer halted, lifted a spear and threw it into the sky like a shooting star. He followed it with his eyes, until it disappeared into the ocean. Startled, the group froze and waited for him to make the next move.

Other natives joined in, until the group was surrounded by dancing natives, wearing grass skirts and tops, woven from large leaves.

Edging towards the dancers, Kidston after Cath waved. With a big smile, he offered his dummy to the tall, dark lead dancer. Jimmelta froze as the natives stopped. dancing. She stared intently at the dancer, awaiting his reaction. The Tank glowered with her arms folded. The family stood motionless. Then the dancer knelt down and patted Kidston's head.

There was a huge sigh of relief from the family and they all clapped, and one by one they shook hands with the natives.

'Welcome, Family Idiot! We have been expecting you and we hope you enjoy your time with us. We are Marmaladians the last living natives of Marmalade Island. We have our own, very beautiful marmalade lava from the beloved Stickiano Volcano. I am King Rindulee and these are my dancers, the Mini Rindulees.'

With that, he bowed and offered the family some food. Jimmelta hoped it would be sweet and sticky: definitely no need for doughnuts.

'Dear King Rindulee, and of course, the Mini Rindulees,' she said, 'may I present my family. Piggers, my adoring husband. My children, Gingham, Paisley, Polka and Kidston after Cath...oh, our tutor, umm, umm... oh, and our dear servants, the Inherited Australian Convicts. Oh, and my adorable camera crew. They're so brilliant!'

A sweeping movement of a handkerchief her hand, wafted in the direction of the family, introduced. They stared at the family, and of course, the golden handbag shaped yacht anchored in the bay. It stood, a glistening garish conqueror, ready to quash any intruder, butting into the near-perfect shoreline, taking the land as its own. The sides of the yacht shimmered and reflected against the waves.

She turned sharply to the crew. The dancers disappeared into the edge of a forest, Jimmelta and asked,

'Did you get it all for the show? Was it exciting for the viewers?' Determined to make this adventure the best thing on television, Jimmelta decided there and then, this island would be the perfect base for her chat show each day. Rather than travel aimlessly, hoping to come across another one, Marmalade Island was perfect.

She had a plan.

She had a very good plan.

And, more importantly, she was proud of herself, she was thinking on the spot- something she normally paid other people to do.

Chapter 9

Although the Jimmi Chew's quarters looked perfect, there were small teething problems. For example, there was not enough water for baths, showers and cleaning food. Paisley solved the problem by swimming in the warm ocean.

He washed with special eco-friendly soap from the Church of Harvey Nichols. The others followed suit.

The evening began well. The Inherited Australian Convicts cooked a lovely meat goulash with vegetables and rice, all rather healthy, but quite dull. Of course, Jimmelta was desperate for a doughnut, but since they were packed deep in the bowels of the yacht, underneath huge boxes of reserves, luggage, and all sorts of welding and building equipment, in case of accident or emergency, it was near- impossible to quench her sugar craving. So, for the first time, she ate a healthy supper served on the deck.

After, the family enjoyed the beautiful calm waters, the children amused themselves playing on the infamous mast. The grown ups stared as the sun disappeared on the horizon. Later, this was followed by some local Marmaladian television. As Piggers turned it on, the remote control in his hands, began to smoulder.

'Do you think the Mini Rindulee dancers broke the cable?' asked Jimmelta very thoughtfully. Wiping perspiration from her forehead, she glanced at her grimacing husband. He wanted to watch the news and cricket with the children, (a rare treat for them now that The Tank was in charge).

'Don't be silly! I thought you'd asked them to be the first guests on your show! Why would they wish to cause trouble? I'll tell you what's happened, that stupid company that built this thing...'

'Yacht, darling,' interrupted Jimmelta.

'Yes, whatever! Well, Pirate Pursuits –

well, they certainly are that! Wiring that doesn't wire, televisions that don't work and air conditioning that doesn't condition! Why didn't you get a reputable company to build this,this, this THING?..'

'Golden yacht,' replied Jimmelta. 'Thing is, Piggers, they were the only company that would take the design and make it.'

'Well, we've only just got here, and look at all the things that are going wrong. I told you not to waste money like this, and what did you do? Use a cheapskate ship building company whose sideline is opening safes and vaults!'

She ignored this final outburst and Jimmelta popped out to discuss the plans for the following morning with the camera crew.

She asked Rooster to tell the dancers about timings for the morning show and make up and then decided to go for a quiet swim. All this arguing was too much, besides, Piggers was right.   She decided a swim or paddle in the wonderful hot sea would be perfect, even though she was useless at it.

The sea was perfect. She felt a moment of bliss, like the warm, bubbly feeling on Christmas morning when everything in the world is wonderful This tranquility was ruined by The Tank, swimming with the full force of her weight, strength and speed.

She decided to ignore the intrusion, and Jimmelta paddled in the water. She watched the dusk slowly turn to dark, as the stars poked through the blackness of the night.

It was all so beautiful, and everything was so dream-like, (except, the pounding of The Tank, aggressively attacking the waves, and shooting fountains of water into Jimmelta's hair).

Later that night, the family went to bed. The children snuggled down excitedly in their bunk beds, and the parents finally fell asleep, thanks to the Inherited Australian Convicts, mending the air conditioning.

Chapter 10

Over the next week the family developed a routine on Marmalade Island. Each morning The Tank woke the children and made them swim across the bay. To begin with, the task was difficult. They hadn't taken this sport seriously, other than messing about in their pool in Bullion Castle's grounds. Filming started immediately. Marjory Stickle Swamp Stick, producer of The Daily Chew, made sure she had plenty of live clips for her viewers back home. She especially wanted film of the three eldest studying being taught by The Tank. It was hard to believe, but The Tank, now had her own fan base as well.

Choking on her first cup of coffee each day, Marjory informed her crew to focus on the children's sporting activities.

'Jimmy John, get right up close and catch what they're saying – I bet it's a hoot! Polka looks the most agile – get a few words from her, then the other two. Oh, and JJ, make sure the footage is funny. I don't want my viewers to see anything normal- know what I mean?'

Jimmy John (the total of the camera crew), jumped onto a waiting speedboat.

He followed the swimmers, filming every attempt to improve their skills.

This exercise was then followed by a 'quick' run around the island , (something Gingham and Paisley hated). Marjory loved watching the footage of this activity.

Marjory was delighted. She knew the tutor (who, incidentally, swam in army shorts and socks), would entertain fans back home, with her continued barking and shouting at the lazy kids. Marjory knew this sort of thing improved the ratings.

Once breakfast finished and the children bathed and dressed, they started work – the 'real' work. And, once again, many lessons were filmed for the audience back home.

In the classroom, the children, who loathed the sessions, were put through their paces with each subject. Times tables, topics in maths, and many more were completed in tears and arguments. The rigour of hard work in all subjects continued to entertain the audience. It was incredulous to watch them struggle with such basic skills in life, such as reading and writing.

Unfazed by her charges' emotions, The Tank ploughed on through each subject, ruling her small but rebellious class with an iron rod. Nobody left her lessons without learning the key points of the subject studied. Paisley screamed, Gingham cried, Polka (by far the brightest), smirked and constantly stuck her tongue out at The Tank, who, consistently ignored it. If they didn't get a problem right, or improve their expression in writing, The Tank added another width to their swimming in the morning. Sometimes, she added an extra lap of the island to their running.

So against all their upbringing, and against their will, they studied at night after eating.

'I can't believe we have to do this. I never worked this hard at school, ever,' wailed Paisley, crying over his long division maths. 'She never lets us do anything except learn. I'd rather go back home to Bullion Castle and back to school. It's horrid here! We don't even get to play during the day with the Mini Rindulees and they look great fun...'

'Yeah, but the thing is, she keeps saying we need all this stuff, if we want to get a JOB!'

All three stood open-mouthed at this. Gingham couldn't remember having a conversation at school, or certainly at home, about such a thing.

'Well, maybe when we're old we'll have to try it out – this work thing,' said Polka, biting the end of her pencil. 'It mightn't be that bad. Look at Mum, she has her own chat show and that's work, isn't it?'

They weren't sure. The Daily Chew revolved around Jimmelta, her views, her favourite people, her clothes, and important national news like, would pink ever replace black and should we have clean, colour coordinated dustbins? This was everything Jimmelta's viewers needed and wanted to know.

However, although Jimmelta was certainly popular, the viewers were fascinated with the children's adaption to their new life on the yacht. They were intrigued how The Tank made their lives unpleasant as possible. The new routines were entertaining for all to watch. The Tank had never seen such weak and pathetic children in her life. The constant arguing and snapping between them entertained her. Whenever they cried about working too hard, she made then do ten press-ups. Very quickly, the children settled down, their moans quieter, their tears hidden and, their voices just whispers. The Tank quietly smirked to herself, when she heard her pupils snivel as they ploughed through lessons each day.

Without fail, each day, the children moaned about The Tank to Jimmelta. They complained of exhaustion, and the amount of work for each subject. Jimmelta horrified, always mentioned this to Piggers, who always chose to ignore it. Piggers was delighted with the new tutor. The Tank was bemused by the parents, as one relished learning, and the other failed to understand its importance for the children.

Only Kidston after Cath escaped the daily torture, too young to swim miles, run miles, read, write and solve maths problems all day.

The others envied Kidston as he played

with the Marmaladian natives. They loved to entertain him. From the workroom on the golden yacht, they watched Kidston toddle in the sunshine. He laughed and played with his toys, with natives in the sea. Paisley, struggled to do long multiplication because he hardly knew his tables. He was distracted when Kidston played with the natives.

'Shh, or she'll make you do press-ups or something,' whispered Polka, looking at a map using the contours to out work high and low land. 'She's completely mad, The Tank, and the weird thing is, she likes, really likes, Kidston. She lets him do anything he wants.' Polka added as she glanced at Paisley, who stared out of the window at the sand, palm trees.

'That's just because he can't walk yet and

he's just a bit more than a baby,' answered Paisley. 'Anyway, it won't last once he's a bit older, you'll see. The Tank will have him reading and spelling before he can talk properly,' he added, as he struggled to complete the maths task.

Planning ahead, The Tank looked at the timetable of activities and lessons, and monitored her pupils' work so far. She growled and snarled like a wolf snatching its prey as she marked. Her thick, black, curling eyebrows knitted, and her cheeks puffed, like red balloons ready to pop, as she read the poorly presented work from her students.

'Gingham! Get over here now and explain what this is meant to say! I can't read it!

What is it meant to be?' The Tank bellowed across the room, and the air from her mouth blew like a small tornado, scuttling paper and light objects into the air. Up to this point, Gingham, shot out of his chair as if woken from sleep. He slipped over his table, bruised his head, and promptly yelped with pain.

At the other end of the yacht, as the sun beamed into her cabin, Marjory watched the action from her seat. As Jimmy John filmed the episode, she smirked. The Tank shouted at Gingham as he did press-ups for his mistakes. With every one Gingham vowed revenge on his tutor, and, possibly his father, for employing her.

Gingham finally continued with his work.

The other two studied, frightened in case they were subjected to the same fate. Polka and Paisley hated Gingham's treatment. They needed a plan ridding them of The Tank. Working under her tutelage was unbearable.

Delighted, Jimmy John managed to get subtle shots of the children hiding their tears from The Tank. For the children, the excitement of the voyage had dwindled down to nothing. Each day consisted of school work, extensive sports and activities until supper in the evening.

At lunchtime the children swam to improve their stamina, whilst The Tank boomed instructions to them- much to their resentment. The Tank studied the weather, she surveyed the skies. Then instructed the children to run when it was cloudy and swim when the sky was clear. A cloudless sky ensured swimming at lunchtime (the lesser evil of the two), and the pupils were grateful for this small mercy.

The tranquility of the island was like a postcard, it was almost picture perfect. Palms swayed gently in the breeze, occasionally bending in a sudden gasp of warm air. The leaves f luttered and sometimes glided down to the sand.

The peaceful image shattered to smithereens as The Tank, instructed her charges at lunchtime, before eating.

The three completed the stretch across the bay most days, as the weather was hot. When it rained they ran up into the mountains, returning to cool in the sea. The exercises guaranteed excellent ratings for viewers. Weak excuses, such as bruised toes, itchy or bitten armpits, rashes or torn ligaments, aches or pains, didn't have any impact on The Tank. After several attempts to convince her of all these problems, the children gave up.

'It's not worth trying to argue about this,' said Paisley, wading into the water and staring out to the other side of the bay, shielding his eyes from the sun.

Polka sidled up to him and also stared. The sportier of the three, she was a confident swimmer across the bay, but was concerned about Gingham and Paisley's lack of stamina. She knew viewers found these episodes amusing, because it made the children look unfit, and lazy.

'Look,' she said, 'to be frank, we have this great sea to swim in, and even though it's boiling hot, we can have fun. Let's have a race to see who can get to the other side first, before she makes us.'

'Yeah, that's a good idea,' replied Paisley, as he gulped at the stretch of water before him. Still recovering from his morning punishment, Gingham nodded in agreement and braced himself for the lengthy swim.

They saw Jimmelta with her guest for today, a Marmaladian fashion designer who used straw and leaves to make clothes and shoes. Polka thought, she looked like a cross between a scarecrow and a clump of compost. However, her mother needed to have unique guests each day on The Daily Chew to maintain high ratings.

'Come on, boys, we'll show the monstrous Tank we can do this without always being bullied or bellowed at. This is our time too! She's got the upper hand every time she tells us off, and we're just falling for it! Let's show the big, fat, stinking lump what we think of her and give her nothing to get at us with!' said Polka, putting on her goggles as she prepared to swim the width of the bay. Paisley nodded, invigorated by the outburst of rage and defiance. Nothing could be worse than the unfair demands. So, determined, he too, got ready to swim across the bay. Gingham, still bristling with hatred toward

The Tank, followed the other two.

By the time their tutor thought to give instructions, they were several hundred metres from the shore. The Tank was amazed. Feeling helpless and redundant, The Tank sat on the sand and stared out at the warm ocean. The Stickiano Volcano rumbled and gently gurgled in the background. The Tank smiled as the children tried to perfect their swimming strokes. Really, she thought, perhaps next time she should join in and challenge them to a race. She aimlessly drew pictures in the sand as she saw the figures in the water become pinpricks in the distance.

Once out of ear shot, Polka spoke. 'Right, you two stop. Just tread water,' she said, and checking over her shoulder The Tank hadn't followed them. 'Listen, this is the only place to talk without cameras and microphones, and away from her. We've got to plan something to get rid of her. We can't let her go on like this –our lives are unbearable. What d'you think?' Polka's statement delighted the boys.

'I hate her! I hate her!' screamed Gingham, splashing his fist into the water as he trod water. The other two nodded in agreement. 'We have to make sure Father sees her for what she really is – a bully! I want to make her do a million press- ups and swim forever...' Gingham took his rage and revenge out on the sea, and giant splashes surrounded the trio. They yelled in agreement at the top of their voices. Suddenly, aware their noise might travel and be heard, Polka swam ahead, beckoning the others to follow.

'I think we should do a series of small things first and make her look stupid. Then, when we're happy about that, we'll think of something else,' began Gingham.

'Yeah! Lots of really stupid things that will make her look really, really useless in front of Dad,' added Paisley excited. 'Let's start with the swimming and show her she can't complain!'

With that, the three swam towards the other side of the bay, cutting through the water, improving their strokes and speed. The group was surprised how exhilarated they felt. The shoreline seemed so far away and their muscles ached, but Polka's voice encouraged the boys to keep on swimming. Their strokes cut the water like knives. The trio were breathless as they swam haphazardly to the shore.

Unaccustomed to the speed of this exercise, The Tank sat on the sand drawing pictures with her fingers and humming to herself. She nodded as they stumbled onto the beach to lie down. Instead of yelling at them to hurry back to the yacht, for lunch, The Tank smiled at them and nodded. She savoured this tranquil moment

- a rare occurrence.

In fact, Polka thought she was ill, Gingham and Paisley convinced she was mad. The sun streamed down, and the children stretched out on their backs. The heat massaged their aches and pains from the intensive swim, soon they nodded off. The image of The Tank casually heaped on the beach, humming and drawing in the sand, completed the calm setting – a rare experience.

'Quick! UP NOW!'

The explosive voice startled the children, and they woke to find The Tank looming over them, her hands squarely on her hips.

'Come on! Now you've had a break you can run back for something to eat. I asked the Inherited Australian Convicts to make something healthy for your lunch.'

The children looked glum at the thought of eating all that green, crunchy stuff.

Chapter 11

Jimmelta struggled with her latest guest on The Daily Chew, much to the amusement of Marjory Stickle Swamp Stick. Under a huge, gaily coloured umbrella on the top deck, Jimmelta splodged on a sun lounger. Opposite, the straw and vine clothes designer, had some natives wearing her Continued Summer Collection. The short, squat, ladies with masses of black, curly hair, proudly wore straw dresses with gathered clumps and battered leaves. They walked up and down the deck, pouting and snarling as they strutted.

Marjory huddled in her cabin, watching the takes, as Jimmy John, the key cameraman, listened to her every command. Another avid disciple of the Church of Harvey Nichols, Marjory couldn't quite work out, where these natives had learnt to do this strutting and pouting. She was sure, based on her treks round the island, there was not an edition of the Catsquawk magazine in sight. So she was bemused when a models bent forward and blew a kiss to the camera. Amazing, Marjory thought, to be out here, stuck in the middle of nowhere, working with natives, only to discover, they were more London than London! Her mind wandered to the scents and smells of London. She suddenly jolted in horror. The designer, named Minso Momo, insisted Jimmelta try one of her 'creations'.

'Do it!' hissed Marjory into an ear piece permanently attached to Jimmelta's ear.

'Why?' snapped a shocked Jimmelta, who forgot she was on air. So viewers saw the beautifully crafted straw garment on the end of her long biro. 'I can't wear this! I set fashion trends, I don't wear gardens...'

'Well, you wore a tractor on your head at the garden party, eh? Remember? PUT IT ON! 'Marjory ordered. 'Why don't you try being ahead of the times with a new style?

Do it now!' The aggressive demand stunned Jimmelta, used to her own way in everything.

'I can't be expected to wear this and sit in it!' gabbled Jimmelta, conscious the conversation was live in Britain.

In the meantime, Minso Momo played with the huge umbrella. As she lifted to close it, the catch snapped and shut like a trap catching a mouse. Jimmelta, screamed at the top of her voice. The designer, quite entertained by the outburst, laughed at her along with the models. 'What have you done?' groaned Marjory. Her head dropped into her long, bony, sharp nailed hands. She growled viciously at Jimmelta, who deafened everyone with her screams which sounded like bullets pelting a tin roof. The producer experienced with dealing with difficult stars, once composed, sat back and watched from the other side of the camera. Far from insisting Jimmelta put the grass dress on, Marjory let the whole episode unravel.

Within seconds, her phone line to producers in head office back in the UK, went on red alert. A bulb lit up every second. Marjory knew from past experience, if a show had poor ratings, the phone would ring at the end of the programme. This immediate connection could only mean one thing: Jimmelta's explosion was good for ratings. When she finally answered, Marjory basked in the praise and compliments from Fred Slobbretto, the new head of television and entertainment in both the UK and USA.

'Hey, Marge, just needed to let you know this fight is something else. I mean, I've been loving the show, I even liked the last one. But Marge, I've gotta say, man, this is, is, is FANTASTIC! Can we get her, this Chew van der Bratt, can we get her to do something like this with most of her guests? The audience is loving it, man.'

Marjory, kept the conversation light and asked what he was doing, still not sure of the voice at the end of the line.

'Are you telling me you don't know who I am? Well, honey, I'm the overall head of the American and UK television network, Spaced Out Television.' There were only splutters and a gulp at the other end. Fred

Slobbretto blew his cigar smoke down the mouthpiece of the phone and cackled. He looooooved making his employees panic as they obeyed him.

He loooooooorvvvvvved his new power! Marjory was no exception. Whilst she was able to dominate Jimmelta with her bullying tactics, she herself, was easily pressurized by those in professional seniority. Marjory patted her hair as she twitched. Although delighted that this outburst was making the ratings shoot up, she was still concerned when her presenter intended to wear the straw and vine clothing. She cleared her throat and answered,

'Jimmelta can be wonderful, but if she decides not to agree to something, she is quite happy to kick up a stinking fuss. I'd really be grateful for your suggestions on how to handle her over this dress.'

Marjory waited for a response from the head of all television –who wasn't listening. He watched as The Daily Chew's viewers ratings rose beating all the other programmes.

'Hey, Marge, yeah, I know she can be difficult, but you should see her ratings. This outburst has put her bang in top position. Number one! I ain't being difficult when I say we have ta keep the girl angry, real angry. Marge, honey, can you fix this?' he asked, his enthusiastic American drawl twanging as he spoke.

'I don't know, Fred. Well, we can see what happens. Do you want me to talk to her?' asked Marjory, as Jimmelta stamped her feet. On screen, the view of Jimmelta squeezed into a straw and vine dress amused, everyone. Jimmy John snorted and tears rolled down his face. This was the funniest sight he had seen for a long time. His 'established' presenter showed a terrible side of her personality. She rudely complained about the fitting and itchiness of the garment.

Jimmelta jumped up and down, turned red in the face and cried at the designer. Minso Momo laughed at Jimmelta's behaviour. Marjory placed the microphone near her mouth, she again snarled instructions to smile and walk proudly in the garment.

Jimmelta numbed by Marjory's fury,

and the stinging words exploding in her eardrums, threw herself into a strange walk. Her head and body twitched. Her arms waved up and down above her head, as if she were trying to catch something in the sky.

'All right! All right! You win!' she snapped, and faced the designer, now perched on the edge of a sun lounger, deep in thought. 'Did you hear what I said?' Jimmelta squawked, her voice hoarse from the screaming. Minso Momo nodded and stood up to face her model. Jimmelta looked decidedly uncomfortable, as she strutted wildly and uncontrollably along the deck. She moved between the beautifully displayed furniture, positioned to welcome and relax guests.

'You like now?' Minso Momo asked, and pointed at the straw and vine dress, which clung to Jimmelta tightly, and made her red with discomfort.

'Well, well, it's not quite what I had in mind to model, when you asked me to wear your new collection. So, well, I'm not sure at all,' responded Jimmelta, trying hard to be polite as Marjory screamed into her ear piece, prompting her.

'Well, I'm not sure what you mean. I saw the hat you wore to the royal garden party this year and how you looked. I think this is better than a tractor, don't you?' retorted Minso Momo sharply. Before Jimmelta could respond, Minso Momo continued. 'Yes, I saw it in the papers and on the internet. So I know this can't be anywhere as bad, can it?'

Jimmelta was clueless how the natives on Marmalade Island knew so much about her. She followed the instructions from Marjory and sauntered up and down the deck. Her huge sunglasses hid her wet eyes and half her face, and tried to muster a smile.

As she pulled her thoughts together, Jimmelta realised that if she wasn't committed to the design, the viewers might feel the same. So she straightened up, composed herself, turned to Minso Momo and said:

'Look, Minso Momo, I think this outfit, beautifully woven from straw and vines, just brings out the animal in me and gives me jungle vibes! I'm sure we could build a dance around this outfit to create a really fantastic impact...' Purring, Jimmelta pleased to wangle out of a difficult situation, praised the design to her viewers.

Minso Momo shook her head in amazement, at Jimmelta's sudden change, after the initial furious and uncontrollable reaction. She stared at her host and tried to think of a reply.

Noting the pause in the conversation, Jimmelta jumped in: 'I think we can have a wonderful programme showing your full collection in an afternoon special. Would you like this? Maybe we can have more details on how the garments are made and what processes take place.' Smiling as she spoke, Jimmelta's enthusiasm impacted on the young designer, who smirked and nodded. Minso Momo wasn't sure if this new appreciation was genuine, or whether it was forced. However, for now, she was delighted to have more coverage on television.

From her seat tucked away in one of the cabins, Marjory looked at the action on deck and chuckled. Never in her wildest dreams had she envisaged giving stern orders to someone with Jimmelta's high profile. She felt powerful, very powerful, so decided to phone Fred Slobbretto and share her news. Her confidence was immediately dashed when reminded that the ratings were high if there was an argument, and, he wanted one most days. Deflated by the reply, Marjory wondered how to make Jimmelta argue with guests. Jimmelta prided herself and made sure her guests enjoyed the experience. She was thrilled when they shared positive comments.

This would be difficult. Marjory sat and poured herself a coffee freshly made by the Inherited Australian Convicts. Marjory was torn, as she wanted to enjoy the show each day, but knew regular outbursts would keep ratings high. She glanced down the list of potential guests for the coming weeks to pick the next victim. She wondered how this demand from Fred Slobbretto could be executed successfully. Jimmy John phoned to say Jimmelta, in an 'intelligent' moment, agreed with Minso Momo, to go into the forest. She wanted to see how the dresses were made. He had to follow behind them and film it all. Marjory pictured the exodus to the forest and wondered if scuffles with the natives improved the ratings. She had to keep Fred Slobbretto happy; after all, he paid her salary.

'Just a minute, Jimmy John, tell me if we can get the odd native or Mini Rindulee to cause a fight or something. Can we get one of the workers collecting the straw and stuff to cause trouble? I dunno, something like a strike. Help me out, Jimmy J.'

She gabbled to her cameraman (who panted as he scrambled to keep pace with the women). Marjory opened the cabin door and shot up to the deck like a bullet. She saw the party disappear into the thickets of tall tropical trees. She saw Jimmy John struggle behind, as he balanced the camera and microphone on his right shoulder.

'Huh, huh, don't knowww. Gosh, I didn't know Jimmelta could walk so fast, it's almost a run! Huh huh,' responded Jimmy John catching his breath.

Marjory stood on the deck, surveyed the disarray left and wondered how to instigate another quarrel between the two women. Not wishing to lose Jimmy John she hurled questions through the microphone. Unaware her cameraman floundered in the forest, amongst branches, tree trunks and boggy areas, Marjory kept firing questions.

Again, it slipped Marjory's mind, the camera still rolled, and the chat was live back home. As she finished the conversation, her mobile rang again. It was Fred Slobbretto's drawling tones. 'See, honey, I said we had something special with this lady Jimmelta. You wouldn't believe how the public are reacting –they're loving it, honey. Just loving it.' He barked with laughter at the antics before him on the screen. Marjory was thrilled to be praised, especially over the unexpected outcome.

'Well, Fred, isn't it amazing how things turn out? Maybe Jimmelta is becoming so wise and good at working the ratings. I don't need to hound her each day...'

'Hang on! Hang on, HONEY! Jus' because she's doin' one thing right, don't mean you can let her decide things! Too much freedom! Honey, you jus' keep doin' what you're meant to do...' responded an irate Fred, determined to keep tight control by whatever means.

'All right!' snapped Marjory, now furious with Slobbretto for his arrogant and condescending behaviour. It was on the tip of her tongue, to tell him that she hated being called 'HONEY'. She decided to leave that piece of information for another day.

Jimmelta and Minso Momo trudged deeper into the forest, and the tops of the trees camouflaged the brilliant bright sky. Only shards of light filtered through. Minso stopped and pointed at a felled clearing. Here, the light shone, opening the surrounding area to a hive of activity. People worked industriously in groups, piling straw into mounds scattered throughout the area. Jimmelta hadn't seen such hard work and excitement since the Christmas sales at the Church of Harvey Nichols. She was very impressed. Transfixed, she asked what all these people were doing.

'Well, Jimmelta, they're taking the grass, straw and vines, collecting them into piles. They're pulling the leaves off the cut trees and drying them out.'

Proud of the industry she was creating, Minso Momo turned to face Jimmy John, who struggled to capture it all on camera. Minso explained how this work gave the Marmaladians a chance to be productive. The women, men and children worked industriously, and Jimmelta was intrigued by everything she saw around her. Maybe her chat show would pioneer a new type of clothing. As usual, Jimmelta's mind began to wander. Already she imagined the headlines in the papers: 'Marmaladian Clothes Hit the Catwalk in Just a Momo.' Grinning at the workers, the cameraman and Minso Momo, and her new friend, Jimmelta, visualised herself promoting new designers across the globe.

Jimmelata watched Minso's workers happily clean and organise the grass and vines, away from the frenzy of activity. Marjory stood on the golden deck of the yacht watching Jimmy John's clips. She stared at Jimmelta's straw clothing, and vowed never to wear them, or to tell her friend, the fashion editor of Catsquawk, about the new creations.

Chapter 12

Once the children returned from their lunch after swimming, they secretly agreed to meet after supper and continue with their plan to get rid of The Tank. A perfect time, when she relaxed after her busy and bossy day. Polka, Gingham and Paisley, now excited and couldn't wait for the evening. For the rest of the school day, the three behaved perfectly: neat work, detailed explanations, a positive attitude towards their teacher, keenness to answer questions thoughtfully, and so the list went on. The afternoon completely puzzled The Tank, now always prepared for an argument, especially Gingham. He was permanently moody and bad tempered. She was taken off guard when he read out his story, and even more flummoxed at voices he created voices for his characters.

'Well, umm, Gingham, I, um, umm, am delighted at such a change in work and attitude. I wonder if we can talk about any developments.' To the pupils' shock, The Tank's voice sounded human - almost gentle. The tone in her voice was, so unexpected.

'Well, I am sooooooo glad you like my

adventure story, about a horrible teacher who is tied up by bandits! THEN tortured on a desert island!' Gingham replied. He emphasised last part of the sentence loudly, and in a tone, making the other two snigger, as they pretended to work.

The Tank squeezed into her huge wooden chair, the fat of her thighs bulged through her clothes, and oozed through the arm rests and back of the seat. Her thick, rubbery left hand rested on the left side of her bulbous chin. It made her cheek sag over the jowl, creating a sullen, grumpy expression. She wiped her heavily lined, and pitted forehead, as the afternoon heat penetrated through the windows. She flicked the perspiration from her hairline, using an enormous handkerchief, which gathered the pearls of sweat and wafted them out into the air. As she lifted her right arm, a mouldy, odorous smell, slithered and sneaked out from the armpit. The stench wasped, and weaved its way through the classroom. Polka and Paisley held their noses tight, as the unsavoury smell circled around their desks, then dispersed into hidden crevices in the walls.

Paisley and Polka read out their creative writing too, using such expression and tone that to an outsider, it sounded like a play on the radio. Again, The Tank was silent. She had nothing to shout about, she couldn't be cruel. She couldn't bellow out the writing didn't sense. She couldn't stamp her feet, and pound the floor like the rumblings of a tornado. She couldn't threaten them with punishments. Their work was too good for any amount of cruelty, and this made her feel bad, sad and mighty annoyed.

After supper Jimmelta regaled the family of her exploits with Minso Momo and the workers, and Piggers shared his thoughts about a new mining venture. The children politely left the table. Jimmy John said goodbye for the night and went off to find somewhere to relax.

'Perfect,' whispered Paisley, following the others to the deck. They heard Jimmelta's voice below as they sneaked into the water. 'Yeah! Remember, there's not much tide, and the sea's the same night and day!' yelled an excited Polka. She was desperate to get rid of The Tank, who now snored in front of the television.

The Inherited Australian Convicts cleared the supper away and began the evening routine checking the yacht for anything suspicious. The natives warned them that pirates were in the area and might be dangerous.

'Fing is, One-Eared Lumpy, them pirates, they don' care if theys hur' ya or stuff like that,' said Rooster, as he filled the dishwasher. 'Tha' King Rindulee, I like 'im. 'E's saying tha' these pirates are dead certain to notice this yach' not tha' ya can miss it, can ya?' The other two nodded; they were also concerned about this news.

'Well, fing is,' said Pinky Squat, 'I don' know if we should tell 'er. She'd probably want to have them on her programme or summit.'

The other two Inherited Australian Convicts agreed.

Pinky Squat smiled and said 'You can never tell wha' Jimmelta's gonna to do.' He changed the subject to King Rindulee who worried the pirates might take their treasure. 'So he's gonna fin' a real good place to hide it. Ya know wha' I said? Well, King, I said, listen, mate, ya can keep it on this yacht.' The other two convicts stared with their mouths open.

'Are you 'aving a laugh? This golden yach' is the FIRST PLACE they'll look!

I mean, wouldn' ya if yous were a pirate? I would!' retorted Rooster, wild with excitement, clenching his muscles.

'D'you fink it's a daft idea then?' asked Pinky Squat, subdued. He'd thought his idea was wonderful.

'Nuts,' answered the other two with their arms folded, standing tall and looking tough. 'Look, Pinky, jus' imagine bein' a pirate. Wouldn' ya like to shave off a bit of this gold, eh? An' don' ya fink yous would see what else there's on board? Fink about it, mate.'

This comment from Rooster made Pinky Squat realise (that although it had been a kind thought to hide King Rindulee's treasure on the yacht), it probably wasn't the smartest move. He nodded and held up his hands in exasperation.

'So, I've been daf' enough to suggest this place. So where could we hide it?'

As the Inherited Australian Convicts discussed other options, the sun began to set and slithers of clouds drifted by in the pink, hazy sky.

Meanwhile, in the next bay three silhouettes huddled together, swimming and sharing ideas about The Tank. They talked about the afternoon and the different response from her when they worked. Only Paisley suggested she might be changing for the better.

This was met with disgust by Gingham, who still recalled the pain of the countless punishments, and told Paisley not to be so weak. The children explored many cruel plans to get rid of their tutor, but each one ended up being dangerous. As much as they disliked her, they didn't want to be held accountable for a terrible or savage act. Polka opened up a new chain of thought and wondered if they should ask the Marmaladians for help.

'What about paying someone to kidnap her and hold her hostage in the volcano? It's just a thought. We could get King Rindulee's people to grab her...'

'And take her to the worst part of the forest...' added Paisley, now excited. 'And tie her up and gag her!'

'Yeah, and the ransom could be for her to be sent back to England,' laughed Gingham.

The children went through possibilities of this working and persuading King Rindulee to agree. Then, staring up at the moonlit sky, they finished their swim, raced back to the yacht, which glistened like a sparkling, luminous, magical shape in the bay. From a distance, they couldn't differentiate the lights on board from the gold. They just blended, and the land looked so black, it was impossible to work out any silhouettes or familiar shapes.

They saw the yacht, and stopped their conversation so it couldn't be recorded, and quietly swam towards it. They still heard Jimmelta chatting to the Inherited Australian Convicts, though were unsure of the conversation. Meanwhile, on the yacht the discussion was grave. The convicts tried to tell Piggers and Jimmelta about the threat of piracy on the islands.

'Fing is, Jimmelta, since The Daily Chew is so popular an' eve'yone knows the yach' is gold an' stuff, well, yous are a target...' began Rooster, who always dealt with any serious issues and problems.

'Well, Rooster, it's very nice of you to be so concerned about our lives and safety. I can honestly say, I've never in my entire life felt so safe. The Rindulees, are wonderful, and they were great when we had them on the show. We've had such good interviews, don't you think?' Then, flicking her hair off her face, ready to smother it with creams, Jimmelta wafted Rooster to the other side of the large lounge.

Piggers, listened intently to the servants' worries. He responded, 'I think it's good you're all so concerned, but I'm sure the fact our yacht's so well known is a good thing. I'll get King Rindulee to send some of his warriors to guard us all tomorrow, and in return we'll do him a favour, something he wants. So don't worry, men, we'll do something – won't we, Doughy?' Jimmelta replied with a worried nod. She hadn't realised the potential problem with the Salami pirates, spotted near the island of Ambergris Caye- not far away.

Out at sea, hidden from view, in a bay of an unhabited island was a galleon.

The huge, wooden, vessel, with alarmingly high sails. It was decorated with images of skulls, and looked like a monster ready to pounce. Here the Salami pirates, (named after their passion for joints of salted meats), rarely strayed from their own islands, the Salami Isles, where the delicacy was eaten most days.

When the pirates wanted a change of food, and they loved to collect the sugary, tangy lava from the Stickiano Volcano. They bottled hundreds of huge terracotta jars, gathering the overflow from the volcano. Once full, they rolled them down a side in the direction of the galleon. The pirates used the lava in cooking and drinks.

The Salami pirates were not known to be cruel. They didn't take sailors, crew, or anyone hostage. So far, nobody had been frightened of them or hurt by them. However, as Rooster pointed out, that was until the pirates heard about the golden yacht, from the coverage in the news. He said it was easy to shave gold from any part of the yacht. So they had to be vigilant at night.

Jimmelta hadn't seen or met a pirate before, and she wondered how one would interview on The Daily Chew. However, she understood the seriousness of Rooster's comments, she said nothing.

The children sneaked back on to the yacht. Once on deck, they said goodnight to their parents. Then, pleased with their variety of plots went to bed, devising ways to kidnap The Tank. From their cabins the children heard the voices of the servants and their parents. Piggers sometimes raised his voice, after a comment or squawk from Jimmelta – all sounded perfectly normal for the family. The children drifted off to sleep, unaware of the events that were to change their lives.

Chapter 13

The children woke early to shouts and screams above on the deck. The sound of boots clambered everywhere, echoing like giant footsteps. Still dozy, Paisley rubbed his eyes and scrambled to the porthole to see the commotion outside. He saw groups of wooden long boats lined up against the yacht, and in them natives pointing spears out towards the calm sea.

Polka lurched towards the porthole in her cabin and saw exactly the same sight: King Rindulee's warriors lined in wooden long boats, standing with spears pointing out to sea. She dressed quickly and dashed up to the deck.

Kidston after Cath was in his playpen, oblivious to the frantic activity surrounding him. Piggers sat next to him with his head in his hands. The Inherited Australian Convicts appeared to be in control, they talked to King Rindulee and his chief warriors. It all looked like something out of a movie.

'What's happened, Dad? Why have we got all this stuff going on?' asked Polka anxiously. Her eyes darted about as she looked for her mother. She could only see the back of Marjory Stickle Swamp Stick huddled deep in conversation with her cameraman, Jimmy John.

'Where's Mum?' enquired Gingham, concerned about the commotion so early in the morning. Piggers looked up at the children with tears in his eyes. He composed his voice.

'It happened last night when we were asleep. I heard nothing, not a single sound. They came down below deck and found your mother watching television after we'd gone to bed and took her.'

At this, Piggers wept, while Marjory, wiped her tears, and filmed the scene with Jimmy John's camera.

'Who took her?' demanded Gingham.

'And what do they want?' As he spoke, his mouth felt dry and he lost his composure. Piggers, pointed to one of the Inherited Australian Convicts for some help.

'Fing is, youn' Gingham, fing is, it's Jimmelta. She's gone missin'. We've 'ad a visit from them Salami pirates las' nigh' when we was all out for the count.' With that, Rooster put his hand firmly on Gingham's shoulder.

The children, too stunned to cry, stood by their father while the servants and the warriors decided their next move. Marjory, meanwhile, was angry because there was no camera footage. Filming stopped rolling in the evening and during the night. She blamed herself for no evidence to help the search for Jimmelta.

'Apparently,' she began, careful to keep her voice even and light, not to frighten the children unnecessarily, 'These Salami pirates are nice and don't hurt anybody.' She stared straight into the children's eyes and finished the statement with confidence.

'Anyway, how do we know it's the Salami pirates?' asked Paisley, gawking at the turmoil on deck.

A thundering voice from the stairs below boomed out: 'They left some salami meat cut into thin slices. It's their trademark.' On deck, to the dismay and horror of the children, The Tank offered everyone toast with jam and a steaming mug of tea. Piggers and the Inherited Australian Convicts thanked her, delighted for something to eat, and of course, a lovely mug of tea. The news plus The Tank's kindness, was too much for Polka – she burst into tears and ran to her father. Gingham, always better after eating when under stress, grudgingly took some toast and tea, and sat down to absorb the horror of the situation. Paisley, shocked, slumped by Kidston's playpen and played with the toys to entertain him.

Piggers beckoned over the Inherited Australian Convicts, who comforted him by pouring more tea. The blue sky, the still blue sea and the early morning sunshine no longer looked appealing to the family.

King Rindulee, appearing fierce, shouted orders to his warriors.

Nobody had ever seen Piggers cry before. Jimmelta was the centre of attention, while Piggers quietly took charge behind the scenes and checked everything was fine. His meticulous attention to detail, continually saved Jimmelta from many scrapes. Even Marjory, not always the biggest fan of Piggers, found it heartbreaking as he cried and felt so helpless. The truth was, Piggers was lost without his wife. Even though she was so annoying, self-centred, arrogant, spoilt and weak, (and so much more, some of it unpleasant); he loved her, and missed her.

'So what happened? I didn't hear anything last night,' questioned Gingham. The children's plans last night regarding The

Tank were now pointless: all that mattered was the safe return of his mother.

Marjory struggled to hold back tears as she filmed the scene. The horror now impacted on the elder children, who clung to Piggers, slumped on a chair lifeless.

'I don't know,' snivelled Piggers. 'I was asleep and didn't hear anyone. She was in the lounge, so I heard nothing.' He fiddled constantly with one of Jimmelta's scarves, knotting and unknotting it, then running it through his hands.

'Didn't you lock the outer doors to the deck?' quizzed Polka, trying to sound logical and calm. 'I locked i' all up, Polka,' answered Rooster.

'I do i' ev'ry night, so I'm sure we is all

safe,' he continued in a crackling and tearful voice.

'We need to call the police,' said Paisley putting an arm around his father.

'I'll help with the search.'

'We all will!' boomed the huge, tornado-like voice of The Tank. Strangely, the children found her loudness comforting and they nodded in agreement.

'We need the police,' muttered Paisley again, his voice now sounded like a whimper. Polka and Gingham agreed.

'There's no police on the island, just King Rindulee and his Mini Rindulees,' answered Piggers. He wafted a hand towards the warriors surrounding the yacht. 'That's all we have,' he added in a listless voice.

'Well, we'd better sort ourselves out and see how we can rescue Jimmelta,' stated The Tank in a decisive voice.

Everyone numbed by the tragedy, appeared relaxed at her decisive approach. Now, the children gratefully accepted The Tank's response. The rest were still too stunned to argue.

Marjory Stickle Swamp Stick ushered Jimmy John to follow The Tank, now engrossed in conversation with the Inherited Australian Convicts and King Rindulee. They listened intently as she spoke. Marjory knew that, although Jimmelta's disappearance was dreadful news, it would make wonderful filming for television.

Her mobile rang and she saw Fred

Slobbretto's number. Marjory wasn't sure she could tolerate one of his enthusiastic conversations at the expense of Jimmelta's safety. So she left it ringing for sometime, as she braced herself to remain composed for the coming conversation. Finally, irritated by the ringing, Marjory answered the phone. She listened to the avalanche of praise for the events unfolding on Marmalade Island.

'So,' drawled Fred, 'did you arrange this disappearance, Marjory? I mean, it's miggghhty good. I just lurvvvvvve the way you've got some reeeeeaaaaallllllllll pirates to help you out with the ratings.'

'Hang on! That's rubbish. I don't know the pirates AND Jimmelta happens to be my friend.' Marjory was outraged by the suggestion the Salami pirates were in on a plot - to ensure ratings.

The unexpected explosion left Slobbretto stunned and, for the first time ever, speechless. 'Look, Marjory, I don't know what to say. I mean, I jus' thought, you know...'

There was a stony silence as Fred tried to backtrack on his assumption. Unused to apologising, the voice petered to a whisper as he wished Jimmelta well. Marjory turned her mobile off and hid it behind one of the sun- loungers.

'JJ, listen. I don't want that man calling me again, so I'm hiding the mobile. I don't want you to answer his calls either. The man's warped and only thinks about money.

D'you understand me?' Marjory's voice quivered with rage at Fred. Jimmy John, so involved in capturing every moment on camera, nodded and continued filming. A furious Marjory went and sat next to Piggers to console him. All major channels gave regular news bulletins and updates.

Chapter 14

It happened during the night when everybody was asleep. Captain Tom Scurvvy edged his eager pirates toward the back of the handbag shaped yacht, which shimmered like stars. Since their arrival, the pirates logged the movements of everybody on board the Jimmi Chew: times for eating, working, resting, routines of the Inherited Australian Convicts: everything.

The Salami pirates were generally quite lazy, and couldn't be bothered to kidnap people and hold them to ransom. As long as they were well fed, life held no danger – until the Jimmi Chew anchored in Orange Bay on Marmalade Island. The pirates rarely ventured from the shores of Ambergris Caye to Marmalade Island, unless it was for the sweet lava from the small volcano. They loved the thick, syrupy flavour, and filled as many kegs as possible. King Rindulee's warriors often helped roll the kegs back to their black wooden galleon. So, it was fair to say, the pirates and warriors got on quite well. Of course, if they could, the pirates would try to steal King Rindulee's treasure. But there were no clues as to where it was hidden, and, were too lazy to hunt for it. Captain Tom Scurvvy merely 'played' at being a pirate on his ship all day long – with his pirates.

But then, the Jimmi Chew, in her sparkling coat of gold, came into the bay early one morning, as the sun was rising. It was a new pirate, keen to impress Captain Scurvvy, who spotted the yacht. Young Bert Belloweather, who was an excellent fisherman, wanted to catch some for breakfast. So, he set off early one morning, in a small, wooden dingy, with only a few biscuits, a bottle of water and a straw hat. He ventured from the island's shores toward the lesser-known ones, when he saw what he thought at first was a sea monster. The arm of the handbag, shaped like a huge pipe or horn, sprouted from the water, glimmering and golden. Initially, he hid at the bottom of his tiny dingy. Thinking if it was, it would glide through the water and pass him.

Then, after some time, Young Bert peered over the edge and saw people walking on it. He realised it was a golden boat. Never, in his life had he seen one in the shape of a handbag moored in Orange Bay on Marmalade Island. The gold reminded Young Bert, of the huge Egyptian statues, once dragged by thousands of slaves.

Young Bert's quest to impress Captain Scurvvy with his catch of fish, rapidly disappeared. He rowed back to the galleon to share the intriguing news. Once told, the pirates wanted to find out if the truth matched Young Bert's description. They waited after sunset, before silently sailing to see, the Jimmi Chew lit up with silhouettes of people roaming on it. Such a discovery, saw Young Bert promoted to Captain Tom Scurvvy's first servant. This meant, caring for his cabin, clothes and food.

This made him the youngest pirate to serve the captain.

Over the next week, the pirates spied on the family, the servants, the television crew and the tutor. They discussed ways to steal the gold without anyone noticing. It was Bert's idea, to swim underwater, and file slithers of gold, from the body of the yacht. Each night, pirates swam deep below the hull of the yacht, to file shavings of gold. Each return prompted a celebration. Captain Tom Scurvvy declared, looting had never been so easy. He had never plundered so much gold in his life!

'Cap'ain, I can't believe we 'ave us a gold boat,' laughed one of the older pirates, as he threw a bag of gold shavings into the air. 'It's like a gift from the 'eavens,' he added clinking a mug of beer, with his fellow pirates.

'Yeah,' added Young Bert. 'It's a weird, like a sea monster. I've never seen anythin' like it...'

'Yacht! Get it righ', Youn' Bert. An' ya righ' because wes caa see i'! So there!' laughed Captain Scurvvy.

The internet provided the captain with a dossier on the Idiot family, Jimmelta, Piggers and the children. The kidnap was an obvious decision, even though it was years since the last one. Of course, in his mind he was determined Jimmelta, his chosen victim, to be the perfect hostage, and he, a wonderful captor. Captain Tom Scurvvy didn't intend to be cruel to Jimmelta and looked forward to meeting her. They wouldn't tie her up. No, she deserved respect.

So, on the fateful night of Jimmelta's kidnapping, the pirates, led by Captain Scurvvy, sneaked onto the yacht and tiptoed down below deck. They found, much to their amusement, Jimmelta in her tracksuit watching television, in the huge lounge far away from the sleeping quarters. Captain Tom Scurvvy slumped beside her on the luxurious, and introduced himself.

'Are you going to hurt me?' asked a visibly shocked Jimmelta, who stuffed two doughnuts into her mouth, just in case these were to be her last.

Determined to stay calm and collected, she asked Captain Scurvvy what they intended to do with her. Captain Scurvvy, an amiable pirate, told her that, she would be fine and not be hurt, but had to get ready quickly. Showing her expertise at shopping like a whirlwind, she stuffed some clothes into a leather travel bag, along with creams, underwear and perfume. Nothing in the world, could be as bad as, her time at Blackpool Illuminations. Here, Snailetta Bottom had publicly humiliated her every day. Jimmelta felt confident, and stuffed her Louis Vuitton travel bag silently, and, with a speed the pirates had never seen. Once it was bulging at the sides, with a few Jo Malone scented candles, nail polish, a few cashmere jumpers, the odd Elie Saab dress, a couple of floaty Valentino linens, plus a few more clothing requirements, she stood ready.

While he waited, Captain Tom Scurvvy slipped the odd picture frame into a large inner pocket in his long coat. The small group of pirates, discreetly picked up any object of a reasonable size, and stuffed it into their sacks and coats. Jimmelta pretended not to notice. While they snooped around the lounge, and tried out the range of programmes on the television, she secretly placed her mobile in the bottom of the bag. She felt quite calm.

Finally Captain Scurvvy whispered, 'Now look 'ere, Jimmelta, we don' want no trouble. We's as nice as pie if yous come quietly. But if yous are difficul', well, I'm likely to be annoyed.'

Jimmelta immediately nodded in agreement, and asked if she could get a few more things, like: her toothbrush, and a couple of jumpers and pyjamas. The pirates stood aghast at the sight of her two, not one, huge travel bags.

'Er, Cap'ain, is yous sure she can have all this? This, is mea' to be a kidnappin'?'

said an older pirate, staring at Jimmelta.

Her arms firmly folded, Jimmelta waited for the designer luggage to be carried. Captain Scurvvy stared at Jimmelta and her luggage, but then he clicked his fingers and sighed. Suddenly, Jimmelta turned to the men and said, 'How will Piggers know I've been kidnapped?'

Thinking about her show, Jimmelta was keen for viewers to note her bravery, she wanted to be seen as a heroine. Jimmelta knew her fans would support and follow the news avidly, waiting for any information about a rescue.

Captain Scurvvy pulled a packet of salami out of his pocket, placed it on the coffee table, and pointed at it. Peering, Jimmelta was horrified to see it cut into thick, uneven slices. It reminded her of spots bunged and sludged together.

Saying nothing, she stood in the doorway and waited to be kidnapped. She was puzzled. She was certainly confused. Weren't her kidnappers meant to frighten and drag her away?

'So what will you do with that salami?' 'Ahh, Jimmelta, it's our mark, y'know, our trademark. They know we've been 'ere. So don' yous worry,' replied one of the older pirates. He put the packet by the side of a scruffy, crumpled piece of paper, explaining everything. So Jimmelta waited for them to finish playing with the channels on her television!

After a while, the pirates went up on the deck, then slid down to a small dingy at the bow of the yacht. It was a struggle for Jimmelta to keep her balance down the ladder to the boat, but she was quite pleased with her attempt. Captain Scurvvy scowled at Jimmelta, and a couple of his men lowered the bags into the dingy. He was already unhappy with his hostage, and, had a feeling, she might be more trouble than anticipated. But, it was too late to change his mind and return Jimmelta. Captain Scurvvy had a feeling of foreboding, as they prepared to set sail.

Within minutes, Jimmelta was on the small dingy heading towards a black galleon. It loomed like a vulture in another bay. She demanded a blanket to stave off the breeze. Then, she asked the men, 'Will I have my own bathroom with a shower and clean towels?'

The time at Blackpool Illuminations loomed heavily in her mind. She still had vivid images of the dirty beds, smelly conditions, and cheap towels and soap from the local stores. The men laughed quietly; this hostage sounded like trouble.

The trip to the galleon wasn't too long and the warm air caressed Jimmelta's face. The moon shone in the black, cloudless sky, and littered it with thousands of pinprick stars breaking through the black seams. The silhouette of the Jimmi Chew, diminished in the distance, its gold vaguely flickering in the moonlight. Jimmelta thought what a perfect photograph the scene would make. The kidnappers, whispered amongst themselves as the yacht disappeared from view.

As they approached the momentous black galleon, they heard the echoes of raucous laughter from the decks –the pirates waited to catch a glimpse of Jimmelta. Although they'd seen her on television, and spied on her every movement, they were still curious to meet the infamous star.

The dingy rested by the side of the galleon, where a rope hung. The pirates used it as a guide for the steps. One by one they ascended. A couple of the pirates carried sacks of stolen objects, thrown to waiting men. Jimmelta couldn't remember if she had climbed a ladder (this was generally left to others). She tried to balance her feet, squeezed into high designer shoes, and still firmly hold her travel bag. Captain Scurvvy noticed her struggle and nudged Young Bert, to help. He immediately grabbed the bag and supported the hostage. She nervously climbed the ladder, carefully nudging her high shoes onto each rung, while her chubby hands, with brightly painted nails, clenched each one.

Once hoisted onto the deck, she met a sea of beady eyes, grubby faces, beards and black teeth, and, a stench that attacked her nostrils and engulfed her. The jeering and shouting stopped, as they stared at their prize, holding her handbag and waiting for someone to speak. A voice from the dingy broke the awkward silence: 'Young Ber' has her, all righ'? You jus' make sure she's all righ'. I'll be up.' Young Bert, stood behind Jimmelta, nodded to Captain Scurvvy and ushered a stunned and nervous Jimmelta below deck. The walk seemed endless, and a pungent smell of oil, petrol and grease, oozed from every spore, cloth, surface and body. It hung heavily in the moonlit air, obliterating the sophisticated, fragrant wafts of Jimmelta's perfume.

She tottered behind Young Bert through the sea of feral-looking pirates.

She'd been kidnapped.

No matter how courteous her captors, they would still ask for a ransom of some sort.

Chapter 15

Back in London, in his office, Fred watched the scenes of the Idiot family unfold on Marmalade Island. He was far from happy. 'I want every channel on all my networks to be focusing on this kidnapping and I want it NOW!' Fred Slobbretto, banged his fat, f labby fist, on to the table for the umpteenth time. His eyes bulged with fury. His channel had to have the best ratings with this news.

'Kid!' he yelled to his researcher, with a cheese and tomato sandwich stuffed in his mouth, while lettuce clung to his lips and glistening teeth. 'Get me Marj, NOW!' The nervous researcher thumbed through the directory of numbers to find Marjory's, then wrote it down for Fred. Back on Marmalade Island, Marjory interviewed family, and the natives, while Jimmy John filmed their anguish. Though the situation was dreadful, Marjory secretly loved the limelight, enjoying, as Fred said, 'a real moment with the viewers.'

However, this new twist on The Daily Chew, was far from pleasant, for the head of American and UK network, Spaced Out Television. He received threats regarding

Jimmelta's safety. In truth, Fred liked the element of danger, it added adventure to the trip, and he avidly followed the unfolding tragedy story on television.

However, a strong group of Daily Chew supporters openly condemned him for the kidnapping, as Jimmelta didn't have body guards. Of course, the executive board not only praised Fred for excellent ratings, but gave hints of further promotion. Fred knew this catastrophe would cement his career globally, and in brief moments, he imagined running for president of the United States. For now, he had to resolve this international crisis, and it needed to be done quickly! As with all tragedies, the television channels ran mini documentaries about the family and their personal histories.

Marjory, in her single moment of international fame, stopped taking calls from Fred. She concentrated on interviews with the family, servants and Marmaladians. Spaced Out Television Centre in Stratford, London, heaved with reporters, and journalists from the newspapers and television channels demanding a statement from Fred Slobbretto. Everyone tried to get past the doorman, Big Diddy, who sadly thought the bribes were a reflection of his popularity. Big Diddy looked at the siege of reporters, and wished he'd washed his greasy and thinning hair.

Of course, the main channel immediately set up a Chewnight special headed by Pernerkity Splonkers, the new political editor. He based himself outside the studios Spaced Out Centre and interviewed everyone.

Fred Slobbretto stared in horror from the window on the top floor, at the press below. They milled about like sharks ready to dissect any victim who dared to leave the building. Added to this, his advisers and researchers put mountains of notes on his desk that demanded his immediate attention. Turning to one of his assistants, he said, 'So why is this all my fault? How was I to know about the Salami pirates? I can't know everything.'

His assistant pushed another piece of paper onto the pile, bowed her head and sidled out of the room. Fred couldn't decide if the lack of conversation was a positive sign or not. Either way, he felt trapped, and waited for the vultures to tear him apart.

Since the early hours of the morning when the news broke, Fred had long discussions with his superiors. He watched the media below worried, as he couldn't work out how the scenario would end. But he knew, whatever the outcome, this would be good for ratings. Outside, by the entrance to studios, leading to the Spaced Out Television Centre, Big Diddy gave an interview to Pernerkity Splonkers. He asked him what it was like to work at the corporation, and, if Fred Slobbretto really was awful and rude, as people said.

Big Diddy, didn't beat around the bush,

especially with money wafted in front of his eyes, and told the truth. He revealed how rude Fred was each morning – how he barked at his people; how grown men ran out of meetings with him; how people hated working with him; and worst of all, his dank, fetid clothes and BO, stinking like a pungent sewer on a hot summer's day. Big Diddy's huge hamburgered frame gesticulated, while his small, squat head shook back and forth. His diddly, squiddly, eyes blinked and watered, as he regaled these stories to Splonkers, who enjoyed the interview very much.

Fred, peered down below. He could just make out Big Diddy shaking Pernerkity Splonker's hand, then waved to him.

Splonkers turned to someone else for an

interview.

A tap on the door disturbed Fred's moment of peace, as an assistant literally fell into the room, and said in a shaky, nervous voice:

'They're on the phone...'

Fred looked puzzled (actually, just more puzzled than normal). He screwed up his nose. 'Who is on the phone? Give me the phone.'

He snatched it from the young girl, who held her nose as she gave him the mobile. Before he could speak, she departed as quickly as she had arrived – in a flash.

A crackling noise distorted the conversation. However, Fred vaguely made out the name, Captain Tom Scurvvy leader of the Salami pirates. He wanted a randsom for Jimmelta. This phone call was Fred's worst nightmare. He struggled to understand how the kidnapper got his telephone number. He took a deep breath and sat down. He felt his hands, cold with fear, and wiped his clammy forehead. He didn't feel in control of a situation. He placed the mobile close to his ear to decipher the words, Fred shook as Captain Tom Scurvvy discussed the ransom.

'Now, Fre', don' yous worry 'bou' Jimmelta, she's doin' righ' fine. But we need a little bi' of money, don' we? Anyway, we's finkin' somewhere abou' a hundred million pounds or there abou's. Anyways, we'll le' you know more.'

The phone went dead.

There was a loud scream.

There was a loud thud.

No reply from Fred: he had fainted on the floor.

He closed his eyes and imagined his life had before this catastrophe.

Chapter 16

Far away from London, on Marmalade Island, on the Jimmi Chew it was chaotic. The children cried, Jimmy John filmed Piggers on his mobile, Marjory had short fragmented interviews with anyone available. The Inherited Australian Convicts huddled in talks with King Rindulee with his key warriors, and the Mini Rindulees offered tribal dances to bring Jimmelta back home.

The Tank looked at maps of the surrounding islands. The idyllic setting envied by viewers everywhere, now reminded them, even with wealth, life could be dangerous. Back on the Blackbird, the Salami pirates decided not to contact Piggers first. They decided to phone the television company for the ransom. Captain Scurvvy, used the knowledge and skills of Young Bert, to find information about the television company. He needed to have a better understanding of Jimmelta's role in it. Young Bert explained the TV channel decided which programmes were the most popular and profitable. As he listened, Captain Scurvvy realised the television company was worth millions! Then he thought of Piggers and his immeasurable wealth, and decided to get a ransom from him too!

On the Jimmi Chew the day was hot stifling, confusing and noisy. Finally, police from larger islands, and military aeroplanes circled the island. Yet, however hard they scanned the waters, jungles and mountains, they struggled to find clues. Jimmelta had disappeared completely. The pirates and their galleon had vanished without trace. Now, the sun, sea and sand appeared cold, soulless and menacing.

A perpetual throng of people continued to crowd the yacht. Many discussed ways to rescue Jimmelta, and ensure no more kidnappings. Marjory John and Jimmy continued interviewing asking for everyone thoughts on on the terrible events.

Many miles away, beyond Ambergris Caye, the pirates sailed into a secluded and cavernous bay. It led to a deceptively deep cove, where stalagmites and stalactites hung, and tipped the cold, dark waters, away from the last of the moonlight. The galleon was maneuvered carefully, then moored by boulders. The air was cold, sharp and smelt like mouldy eggs ready to be thrown away. On deck, the men waited to hear from Captain Scurvvy.

Jimmelta, in the meantime, was asleep in a comfy and rather old-fashioned bed, with a heavy quilt. Her new cabin was tiny – so tiny, her travel luggage couldn't quite fit in, so propped open the door.

In a state of shock and in the dark, she saw nothing much of her surroundings. She missed the dead rat under a stool; a blanket covered in oil and grease on the bunk bed; and, a series of nuts and bolts scattered across the wooden f loor. This was covered in a film of dust, grease and mouldy food.

Once their hostage was out of sight, the pirates went below deck to have a sleep. Of course, unlike the space of the Jimmi Chew, the cabins were cramped; only thin planks of wood, nailed together in an ad hoc way, separated the sleeping quarters. Jimmelta's slumber was disturbed by snoring, yelling out, burping and snuffling noises from the men. This was something she hadn't encountered, since time   at Blackpool

Illuminations. Automatically at seven o'clock next morning, she woke up to a pitch-black cabin. Confused, she stumbled across the nuts and bolts, clambered over her travel bags, still oblivious to the stench, and the other disgusting things. Edging down the long, narrow corridor, past the cabins of snoring pirates, she recognised the outline of the steps leading to the deck. Carefully, in her pink cashmere socks, she placed one foot at a time on each rung, gripping the rail to support herself.

Once on deck, she struggled to gauge the outline of the galleon. The tall mast and sails, thick ropes, trunks, heavy equipment, brought home the horror of her life at this moment. In theory, Jimmelta knew it was light, it was daytime, yet here in the depths of the cave and lagoon, it was completely dark, almost like nothingness, just black. Suddenly, a torch shone in her eyes, and startled her, and she sat down on something that felt like a box.

'Ere, wha' yous doin' here? Cap'in Scurvvy'll get righ' mad if yous don' do as yous told,' a gruff voice said as the torchlight beamed into her eyes, dazzling Jimmelta.

'Well, ummm, in theory I know it's morning, and it should be light, so I woke up to get up and have some breakfast. But it's soooooo dark. I need some light and can't find it,' she answered firmly. She was determined not to weaken, just because it was dark. 'Anyway, why is it so cold and icy? I thought we were in a hot climate. I don't understand what's happened why are we here? I'd like more information.'

She pushed the torch away, and saw the outline of a heavily, lined face, and beady eyes glinting. The pirate told her to sit down and be quiet, as everyone was still asleep.

So she did. Somehow her instinct, generally poor, told her to be quiet. Eventually, bored and cold, she nodded off. She dreamt of her soft, clean sheets back on the Jimmi Chew, their floral scent soothing her as she slept.

Yells and laughter echoing in the caves broke the sleep. Jimmelta squinted to see the pirates walking towards her on the deck. 'Why you out' of your cabin, gir'? You be quiet an' good,' whispered Young Bert, who had orders by Captain Scurvvy to stay close to the hostage.

'Well, umm, I woke up, thought it was morning, and found it all really dark. Can't we have a bit of light?' she asked Young Bert, who checked the sides of the galleon with the other pirates.

A gun shot from the top of the mast shocked everyone including Jimmelta. She ducked behind some tarpaulin, shaking, as the voice of Captain Scurvvy echoed through the cave, instructing the men to gather. Peering from undercover, Jimmelta saw the men clearly as they shone torches. They listened to their master, who sat on the mast. Jimmelta was most impressed and thought he must be an acrobat in his spare time, when he wasn't being a modern day pirate.

'Men, we got us a nice bi' of money with our Jimmelta,' he shone his torch down on the figure covered up. 'Now we knows Jimmelta is a nice lady, an' I spoke to her boss in England, Fred. We will look after her real nice, and all you men will be polite. Now, I know Jimmelta might wan' fings a little clean, so, men, we'll do that righ' now. I will talk to 'er family later on after we've all eaten. Men, to work now!'

Amongst the roar of laughter and general chaos, Jimmelta watched the men in amazement as they obeyed their orders and tidied up. The lagoon filled with the men washing and cleaning their clothes, singing and whistling, the noise trapped by the thick, limestone walls. Not feeling remotely frightened now, and used to the light from the torches, Jimmelta wandered around the deck of the galleon. She watched the men engrossed in their chores. She worried about her family back on the yacht. They would be frightened and concerned about her welfare, plus, she needed to let them know she was all right. At the moment, the Salami pirates were fine, quite friendly in fact, and being held hostage wasn't too bad.

Captain Scurvvy, below deck, sat at a large, grubby oak desk, strewn with everything from, paper to food cartons, to bicycle inner pumps, to dirty plates. Determined not to comment on this mess, Jimmelta sat down on a mound of squashed cardboard boxes, piled on a low stool, crossed her legs and folded her arms, and stared at him.

'So, Jimmelta ,wha' can I do for ya? We'll be havin' some food an' stuff soon, but doub' if we can ge' you a doughnut! So have some frui', here,' he said, passing her a bowl of overripe plums, creased and shrunken with the heat.

She took one, and rubbed it clean, and pondered, before squeezing the fruit into her mouth. Her eyes closed, as she savoured the succulent sweetness, of the thick, sugary juice, which squelched and slithered, as it circumnavigated her mouth. She caught the trickles of juice on her fingers, and licked them until the taste was gone, and then folded her sticky hands.

'Captain Scurvvy, I must say the men have been fine and it's wonderful to see them working...'

'They're cleanin' for you, so you is 'appy to be 'ere,' said Captain Scurvvy.

'Well yes, I appreciate this. It's all wonderful being here with the Salami pirates. Can I phone home? And, as a matter of interest, how much have you asked the TV studio for as my ransom? I imagine it's quite a lot,' she added, determined to keep her voice light, positive and cheery. Captain Scurvvy stared at Jimmelta. She appeared so confident. From under his pirate hat, his lips tight he answered.

'A 'undred million quid,' he said quietly. Catching her breath at this sum, Jimmelta thought before she spoke, something she rarely did. She speculated if that was a lot of money. She considered the bags of gold shavings, dotted around the galleon, each with a weight on it. She wondered how long it would take to shave away part of the yacht. She shuddered, then thought about a hot bubble bath with her special scents from the Church of Harvey Nichols. Then, the reason for the talk 'popped' back into her head.

'Captain Scurvvy, I would love to phone Piggers, and tell him I am fine, and you're all being so nice to me. I do like your Salami pirates, they're very nice –though a little noisy,' she added quietly, surprised by her calmness. Captain Scurvvy listened to her request and said he would think about it.

Back in the mess room, the pirates ate meat, fruit and lava from the volcano on Marmalade Island. Once ensconced with the men, Jimmelta relished the lava on her food – she had never tasted anything like it. She wondered why the Inherited Australian Convicts hadn't found this delicious, sweet food. Once full to the brim, with meat, lava, lava and more lava, Jimmelta sleepily went back to her cabin. She had a shower in the smallest space she had, ever seen, and change into warmer clothes.

As she rested, she wondered if the kidnapping had made the papers. And, she pondered how Marjory was producing her show. She thought about her faithful and kind Piggers, who would be confused and so unhappy.

Then, she fell asleep.

Chapter 17

In Russia, the man with an even larger yacht than Jimmelta, watched the news on his golden television. Recalling his conversations with Piggers, about the dimensions of the Jimmi Chew, he remembered him as a likable man. So Oli Gark concerned about Jimmelta's kidnapping, wanted to help Piggers. The billionaire made his wealth by discovering syrup, oil and diamond mines in the Volga Urals, and used his power to expand his wealth. He now had everything in his life. Oli Gark was depicted as, ruthless, demanding the biggest and best of everything in the world. Occasionally, he was kind. Every now and then, he showed some compassion. He remembered the last conversation with Piggers, regarding his yacht. Oli's was bigger than Jimmelta's, and didn't care what she thought. He found it odd, when people said positive things, and bestowed gestures on strangers. He watched Jimmelta's show, and was surprised at the flood of generous offers, from viewers across the globe, to raise money for any type of rescue. Oli suddenly realised that, whilst he was one of the richest men in the world, he had no family,

no friends,

no pets,

just countless people, who obeyed every request and command. Oli doubted if anyone would think to rescue him if been kidnapped.

So, Oli found himself in an unfamiliar situation, wanting to help another person in trouble. He decided to ring Piggers, who had been so helpful, and happy to oblige him. In return, Gark and his soldiers would propose a rescue mission. On the phone that night, he shared his plan to rescue Jimmelta from the Salami pirates.

'The zhing Piggers, I am sure my Svwat Teamz can help you. I remember how you gave me zee dimenzions of ze yacht, so now I helps you.'

He was surprised how easy it was to say something kind and thoughtful. He listened to Piggers' snuffles and tears over the phone.

'I am sure thatz I can find her. I will flyz out on my gold jet witz black diamondz and see what the Svwat Teamz can do. Hang on Piggers, ze are coming to zee rescue! Furthermore, I don't even mindz about zee gold yacht now I 'ave zee goldz planez. So wez are equal now, eh, Piggers?'

Piggers, thrilled by the gesture, agreed that Oli could stay on the yacht.

The children were excited about meeting Oli Gark, as they had never seen a cruel, ruthless billionaire before. They had only heard their mother say how terrible he was. They imagined his arrival, with his personal army, 'zee famous Svwat Team', fearless in their protection of Oli Gark.

Piggers was grateful for any help to find his beloved Jimmelta. He imagined her chained up, blindfolded or made to scrub and clean for her captors.

'Cor, with the police now, and Inherited Australian Convicts, they should find her really quickly. Plus, the Svwat Team are really dangerous! They never smile and have the biggest muscles in the world,' said Paisley, brightening up at the news. Marjory planned an interview with Oli Gark their new saviour, and discussed with Jimmy John what to wear for the momentous occasion. The Tank tried, (with little luck) to get the children to work. 'What is he like to know?'

Polka asked Piggers, who attempted a smile.

Piggers didn't like Oli at all, and knew he was cruel. But maybe his characteristics were exactly what was needed to rescue Jimmelta.

'Well, he's not really my sort of person and we don't have much to do with him. It was Oli Gark who wanted to have a bigger yacht than the Jimmi Chew. Your mother didn't like that at all.'

Polka and the others nodded. The thought of their mother being angry made them wince.

'So what does he do?' questioned Gingham, 'Is he sort of a bad and good guy at the same time?'

'He can be dangerous if people let him

down, or don't do as he says. Then he can be fine other times. However, he is not, not, not a kind or thoughtful person. So if he's helping, there must be something he wants from me, something he's going to take.'

The group fell quiet. The excitement of the rescue was replaced by the worry of a potential demand. Unknowingly, Jimmy John had their conversation on film, at Marjory's instruction. She was nervous at meeting someone more horrid than Fred Slobbretto. The silence broke at the sound of booms and screams, from the Mini Rindulees, beginning another tribal dance for Jimmelta. This time they asked their gods to keep her safe until Oli Gark arrived.

In the meantime, the Inherited Australian

Convicts practiced exercises to save Jimmelta, away from everyone on board. They followed The Tank's instructions and used sand ballasts as weights. The children found it hard to cope, but were secretly pleased by The Tank's new vocation. She trained the servants for battle, to save Jimmelta. They looked on as Rooster, One-Eared Lumpy and Pinky Squat struggled to keep the ballasts on their shoulders whilst perfecting their lunges. They tried to keep up with The Tank's instructions.

As the sun set, Piggers and the children sat snuggled in the large, television room, and watched the news. They cried at the headlines about Jimmelta's kidnapping. Police officers flew from England, and message from the prime minister, Horatio Bumbsworthy-Fudge, implied they would find Jimmelta very soon.

Then came further news. The head of Spaced Out Television, Fred Slobbretto, finally broke his silence about the ransom. He told viewers the Salami pirates, 'just' wanted a hundred million pounds. Slobbretto looked down at the ground and whispered, that although, the fans and nation loved Jimmelta, the corporation didn't have the money, so were at a loss. The children sat quietly and stared at Piggers.

'Well, we could give them our boat or yacht, whatever it's called,' Paisley sniffled. 'I mean, I'm not bothered by all this gold an' stuff. In fact, I'm happy with nothing at all. I just want our mother back.' The others nodded and waited for Piggers to say something, to quell their anguish and grief. He hugged them and said nothing. However, he was determined use Oli Gark and his team successfully, once they landed. He hoped for something positive to turn their fortunes around. Of course, Piggers had the money, but the ransom clearly was meant for the television company in London. So now, he was reliant on Oli's petrifying Svwat Team.

The family listened to the rest of the interview on television. Fred Slobbretto faced the camera and said the company intended to find the money from other sources. He promised to contact Piggers and give his support.

Back in his palatial four-storey penthouse in Moscow Russia, Oli Gark finalised his rescue mission for Jimmelta. He ensured his team were ready for an early start the following day. He leaned back in his large, soft, leather, diamond- stud chair and smiled. For the first time in his entire career, as one of the most feared and richest men in the world, with power and acquisitions in every corner of the globe, Oli Gark was doing something wonderful: he was going to save Jimmelta. Somehow, this decision made him happy.

Chapter 18

On the Blackbird, and now accustomed to the darkness, and sharp air, in the hollow of the cave, Jimmelta was quite at home with the pirates. They were friendly and cooked her meals. She smothered her favourite accompaniment, the thick sweet, gooey lava from the volcano, on all her food, to make it edible. Intrigued, by the sugary substance, tasting like orange marmalade, Jimmelta decided to get tonnes once she was free. Since her arrival, the pirates, keen to impress and make her welcome, cleaned their clothes, and scrubbed the decks. However, the thin wooden planks for walls, made it impossible for her sleep. The snorting, snoring, snuffling, gruffling and burping, from the pirates disturbed Jimmelta's slumber.

Captain Scurvvy always invited Jimmelta to join the pirates at mealtime. She sat on the most comfortable chair, a wooden crate propped on bricks with sacking, stuffed with straw to form a cushion. Jimmelta wisely accepted the attempts from the men to make her feel comfortable. After dinner, Captain Scurvvy relented and decided that she should call Piggers and the family.

'Here you are, gir', have the phone, an' don' take long.'

He threw his mobile across the long, thin, wooden, table to Jimmelta, who yelped with joy. She shot out of her seat to grab it with both hands.

'Oh, thanks! That's just brilliant!' she shouted back. Her eyes brimmed with tears, at the thought of speaking to her beloved Piggers and, her darling children. Tentatively and clumsily, she phoned, and her whole body shook as she tried not to cry.

'Piggers! Piggers, it's me, Jimmelta! Yes! Yes! I'm fine. The Salami pirates are being very kind to me and are actually really lovely people. Well, I know it's horrid, this ransom, but honestly, I am having a good time. Yes, of course I miss you all and can't wait to get back to the yacht with you all. Anyway, d'you want to speak to Captain Scurvvy?'

Much to the amusement of the pirates, listening to the conversation, Jimmelta walked over and handed the phone to Captain Scurvvy. He hadn't expected this. Embarrassed, he shuffled on his seat, scratched his forehead, and coughed to clear his throat. Then, he gingerly took the phone and spoke to Piggers.

'Err, is i' Piggers? Umm, umm, well good t' chat t' ya 'bout Jimmelta. She's doin' righ' fine, an' we're all fine here. So, Piggers, 'bou' this money. A few million an' we can forge' about all this trouble,' said Captain Scurvvy politely. Piggers, thrilled at the conversation with his wife, listened intently to the other voice.

'Hello, well, I'm glad you are being kind to Jimmelta. We're all missing her very much, and her public miss her too. I have to tell you, as it's on every television that, one of the richest men in the world, Oli Gark, is at this moment sending his team of men to track you down. He's really not very nice, and can be cruel. Captain Scurvvy, I can't help. I think the best thing you can do is give Jimmelta back. We can forget about this incident.'

Piggers sounded quiet, but very decisive. Captain Scurvvy hadn't heard about Oli Gark and his Svwat Team rescuing Jimmelta. He had no idea who he was! To quell his nerves, he slurped a cup of lava and licked his sticky lips.

'Well now, Piggers, I hope you're no' tryin' to scare me? We Salami pirates ain' afraid of anyone, see...'

'Captain Scurvvy, you don't understand, this man's private army will spare nobody. It will be better if it was sorted now, and we forgot all about it. The team is known worldwide. I can't tell you how horrid it's going to get.'

Piggers paused, and waited for a response. He heard a cough at the other end of the phone, followed by whispering.

'Well, see here, Piggers, I'm gonna give this a real big thin' an' maybe ge' back to you.'

And Captain Scurvvy handed his mobile back to Jimmelta, who, like the rest of the pirates, was speechless at the conversation between the two men. After a few words and kisses blown down the mobile, she closed the conversation and gave it back.

The pirates looked at Captain Scurvvy. Pensive and quiet, he left the table and walked out on deck to think. He didn't want to get into a serious fight with a proper group of soldiers. He stared back at his men, they couldn't stand up to this aggression. The pirates never hurt anyone, and his men were getting old. He rememberd the fun over the years with them. He recalled the parties, the pretend lootings, the adventures at sea on their galleon, and, the mountains of lovely, gooey lava. The plan to make money from his hostage appeared to be in jeopardy.

'So, Capt'in, wha' we's gonna do? Do we give up this 'ere Jimmelta or wha'? Do we want trouble with this team?' asked an older man, who moved around with great difficulty, and worried.

Captain Scurvvy surveyed his men, intently waiting for an answer. As he gazed around the room, he saw Jimmelta kneeling by a barrel, shovelling huge spoonfuls of lava, greedily into her mouth, oblivious to the discussion. Jimmelta was just so happy, now she'd spoken to Piggers and reassured him that she was fine. Her mind drifted away to hot baths, clean, fluffy towels, whilst her body drifted towards the sticky, gooey lava that she loved so much. It was all going to be fine, she thought, as the final scoop slithered down her throat, tickling the sides, as it trickled down to the homely place in her stomach. Piggers would save her. Captain Scurvvy would stop being a pirate, and sell the gold shavings from the yacht. The Tank would sail away on the galleon. And Jimmelta's show would stay at number one forever!

She mused over the various perfect options how these events would play out. Jimmelta didn't hear a helicopter, or a loudspeaker, shouting out her name above the island. The pirates were silent. Helicopters now circled the islands, focused on rescuing Jimmelta and searched.

The loudspeakers called out her name in the vicinity of Ambergris Cayc and Marmalade Island. Miles away in her thoughts, Jimmelta failed to see the pirates make their way below deck and close the hatch whilst they decided their next move. They had to decide how to deal with the Svwat Team.

Being the perfect hostage, once she realised she was on her own, Jimmelta walked to the hatch, knocked on the door and asked to be let in. Then she waited obediently in the dark. From this position, the entrance to the cave was a blue pinprick, and a thundering helicopter flew over the sea. She really wished to have some sunshine, and hoped the galleon drifted towards the entrance, so she could enjoy the heat.

Below deck, the pirates argued about the best course of action. Nobody thought a serious Svwat Team, would lead the rescue.

Wishing to know about them, Captain Scurvvy made Young Bert do an Internet search. When the boy squealed in horror at the information, the pirates froze. Reading slowly, Young Bert shared the facts about Oli Gark, his money, his formidable power, and his private army, the Svwat Team. Captain Scurvvy and his men listened. Not a word was said. This was not the man, or team, to make your enemy.

Chapter 19

The thudding engines and propellers sucked the air in and spat it out. The sea sprayed, trees bent, and the sand blew like the remainder of a Saharan storm.

This was the first indication the Svwat Team were about to land. Six gold plated helicopters approached Marmalade Island. Each, like a shooting star gliding through the sky from a distance. Closer, more like miniature suns falling, they circled the beach near the Jimmi Chew. Then they lowered to settle on the beach.

Marjory and Jimmy John filmed the dazzling entrance. The Mini Rindulees gasped at the enormous structures, which dominated the beach. The children, The Tank, Piggers and King Rindulee goggled at the beautiful gold swathing the helicopters.

It went silent. They all waited. The helicopters stood still.

Suddenly, swarms of men jumped out and stood to attention facing the shoreline, all heavily armed and clothed ready for duty. Piggers stared at the severe group, and hoped Captain Scurvvy understood the implications of this kidnapping. Having spoken to him, Piggers realised the pirates were harmless, and wanted a bit of money. However, Piggers was extremely grateful to Oli Gark for offering his support. The police from other islands, did not seem effective so far.

Heading the team was a short, round man with a bald head and a black, curly, moustache. Oli Gark. He marched towards the yacht. Piggers peered down to the rescue party, standing to attention on shore facing the yacht.

'So Piggers we are here for you anz your family!' shouted Oli to Piggers, and saluted him.

The children, slightly terrified of this man, prepared to help them, smiled. Piggers beckoned Oli Gark to board his yacht. First, he greeted Oli with a hearty hug and a handshake. 'Oli, how wonderful of you to come and help me rescue Jimmelta. We're not having much luck with the local people here, or the police for that matter.' Piggers repeated the situation as he guided his guest below deck for privacy. Then they bowed their heads together, deep in discussion to prepare a rescue. The team stood motionless below, not moving a muscle, waiting for orders.

The children followed silently. The Tank stood still on the deck with the Mini Rindulees, not sure what to expect. Jimmy John filmed Oli Gark's dramatic entrance, and tried to sneak behind him below deck, but was politely shooed away by Piggers.

Below, on shore, the Svwat Team continued to stand to attention, like statues. There wasn't a flicker from their eyes, not a smirk, not a sound at all.

'So Piggers, we have already flown allz aroundz the islands withz not a clue about Jimmelta. Did youz hear uzz? But I have my wonderful jetz and I promise wez will find her.'

Oli waved his hands in the air and showed his appreciation for the golden yacht. In his eyes, it was the ultimate in excellent taste. Piggers proudly recounted the details of the dodgy shipbuilders; the trouble in the Thames, the yacht blocking traffic; the summons from the Queen; the Tank, the children's tutor; landing at Marmalade Island; the chat show; Marjory and Jimmy John; and many more details. Luckily, the men talked in privacy, away from the camera crew.

In the meantime, the children watched the Svwat Team, still standing to attention on the beach. Rooster, decided to walk down and greet them.

'Well. We are real glad to sees you 'ere and wondered if you'd like some water or somethin'?' he asked. The soldiers stood in the line, looking ahead. Their eyes barely blinked in the sunlight.

A voice yelled from the deck, and Rooster saw Oli survey his team and golden helicopters. He peered down at Rooster, holding a jug of water, and shouted to his men.

'Menz you can eat and relax. So enjoyz yourselves! We havez work to do tomorrow!' The team put down their firearms, took off their heavy armour and chatted to each other. The soldier near Rooster grabbed the water, smiled, and glugged it down as fast as he could. Gark's men were hungry, hot and very thirsty, so Rooster, the children and The Tank brought more water to the beach.

The men relaxed; some went for a swim in the warm water. King Rindulee called his warriors and told them to help the team. They took fruit and nuts down to them, along with the famous lava.

Marjory Stickle Swamp Stick knew this

was an opportunity to interview the men. She demanded Jimmy John mingle with the team. Once fed and watered, the Svwat Team lay on the beach. Any interviews were impossible as attempts to speak English were limited.

Below deck, Oli Gark planned Jimmelta's rescue with Piggers. Piggers knew Captain Scurvvy wasn't aggressive and wanted his life spared. From the conversation, he deduced the pirates were not dangerous, and an incentive would release Jimmelta. Oli sniggered, he always fought hard in battles, rescues and invasions. He didn't want anything to change now. However, he respected Piggers's request. Jimmelta was his wife.

The children were delighted with the turn of events. Not only was their mother going to be rescued by these powerful men, but The Tank forgot about school work! The children loved the golden helicopters and took a closer look. In return, some of the team admired the Jimmi Chew and her unusual shape. Oli and Piggers drew up plans to rescue Jimmelta, and Marjory and Jimmy John, secured photos and film of the Svwat Team relaxing.

The children felt safe. King Rindulee and the Mini Rindulees tried communicating with the Svwat Team, as they enjoyed their break with the natives.

Finally at the end of the day, the sun set and the group danced around a campfire.

Everyone followed the Rindulees' actions. King Rindulee told the children the war dance would bring Jimmelta safely back to her family. So they all danced hoping the magic was successful. The children frolicked until the stars glittered in the sky, and everyone disappeared into the night.

Marjory knew the viewers back home would be mesmerized by the bizarreness of the day. How many people travelled in gold helicopters with their own guards? Marjory couldn't think of any. Of course, Marjory couldn't engage with the viewers like Jimmelta, or imitate her lifestyle. Still, the kidnapping ensured millions tuned in for the latest progress report.

Piggers and Oli Gark still discussed

Jimmelta's impending rescue.

'...Zo we will put the menz in the secret submarine and search for ze shipz, then send in ze others to rescue her. Eh, Piggerz, is this right? What do youz say?'

'Perfect, Oli! I like the idea of the submarine very much. But I we'll tell Marjory Stickle Swamp Stick to stop filming. Better still, we'll lock away the cameras. We don't want to lose our bargaining rights with the public! So we'll tell her not to film tomorrow. I'll phone her now...'

Marjory and Jimmy John trudged down the stairs to see Piggers. Each carried film equipment, not happy to meet with Piggers and Oli. Marjory sulked and scowled as she knocked on the door.

They slid away once told not to film the rescue. They knew the mission was important and wondered if the plans would succeed. They hoped Oli Garks' team would not disappoint!

Chapter 20

Captain Scurvvy was worried about Oli Gark's team.

'Fing is, Capt'n, we's the Salami pirates an' we need to 'ave a bi' of power,' said one of the oldest pirates. 'We all like this 'ere Jimmelta, bu' we fink we should make her work a bit. Ya know, to add a bi' of drama an' stuff.'

Captain Scurvvy listened to Old Triggers

who spoke. In the corner, Jimmelta sat and ate another drum of lava, once again oblivious to the conversation.

'I know wha' you mean,' he replied. 'So what are we gonna do? Look at her, she's so happy eatin' all tha' lava. We ought to do something, especially since we have that golden Russian with his big, fat golden helicopters. Tell you wha', men, leave it to me...' Captain Scurvvy dismissed everyone except Young Bert. His servant scoured the Internet for any more information about the Russian and his team. Captain Scurvvy intended to hatch a plan which would save them from Gark's fate.

So much information, so little time to devise a plan, to leave both Piggers and the children desperate. He grabbed Bert, gave a huge smile and shared his plans concerning Jimmelta.

'See, obviously, Young Bert, we'll 'ave to make her 'er work on the decks, scrubbin' an' cleanin'. Now she won't like this a' all. Then we takes 'er to the volcano on Marmalade Islan', an' we gets 'er to gather the lava into barrels. She can roll them down the hills, an' put 'em into small boats, then row to our Blackbird. What d'you fink, Young Bert?' Captain Scurvvy questioned. He clapped his hands and smirked with glee: nobody would say he was a weak, gentle pirate now.

Young Bert finally looked up from the laptop, white as a sheet. He was unimpressed by Captain Scurvvy's speech. He said quietly: 'Look 'ere, sir, I said before we 'ave trouble.

I finks we've a lo' of trouble with this Oli Gark, he's Russian and owns everythin'. He's a friend of Piggers, an' worse...' He paused, ensuring he had Captain Scurvvy's full attention. 'Sir, much worse is the Svwat Team...'

He gabbled on, quoting from the Internet about their strength, power, victories, rescues and missions. Captain Scurvvy perched by the long wooden table, his legs propped on a stool, his face pensive, as he listened to Bert reel off the information.

'...The Svwat Team, valiant, dangerous, fearless and emotionless, can, in a split-second, break through the most troublesome, dangerous groups to catch the culprits and bring them to their knees before Oli Gark.

Nobody has yet escaped the clutches of the Svwat Team...'

Young Bert turned to Captain Scurvvy, and looked appalled. This kidnapping was meant to a little fun with the Salami pirates. Worse, he quite liked Piggers, who seemed decent. However, Oli Gark was serious, and his Svwat Team could easily capture the old, pirates.

No, the facts were not good news.

Captain Scurvvy knew he had to save his men from the Svwat Team, plus, make Jimmelta's life a bit tougher. After a discussion with Bert, he decided Jimmelta would be moved during the night by rowing boat to a cove. Then, when instructed, to the volcano ready to collect the Stickiano Lava.

In another cove, the pirates would prepare to fight the Svwat Team, with lava cannon balls that would stick to everything.

'Well, sir, we 'ave to tell Jimmelta our plans, so she's understanding about it all,' said Young Bert, closing the laptop. 'We could jus' get tha' chap Piggers on the phone an' ask him to come an' get her.' Captain Scurvvy shook his head, so Young Bert fled to find Jimmelta.

Jimmelta, was 'relaxing' in her cabin. To stop worrying, she concentrated on things such as her beauty routine each day. She tried not to think about the ransom of a hundred million pounds. She 'knew' the television company would pay it. No. She was far more concerned with her face cream, which hardened on her skin in the icy air. The Church of Harvey Nichols failed to mention this fact. She longingly imagined the scents from the store, the aromas which surrounded her. The magical fragrances filled her mind with floaty, golden images. Unable to concentrate for a sustained period of time, Jimmelta's mind switched to The Tank, the repugnant lump hired to educate her children. Once free, back on the Jimmi Chew, she vowed to have her replaced.

In her grubby cabin –swept and dusted by one of the pirates, a dank, mouldy and a rather putrid stench filled the air. Jimmelta found a scent in her bag and sprayed it. She focued on being positive, not morose, and thought about her captors. So far, she was content: the pirates were kind, and kept her supplied with the sweet sticky lava from the volcano. It tasted marvellous, though, was not too good for her waistline! Everybody here, was kinder than her experience with Snailetta Bottom and Reggie at the Blackpool Illuminations. This was a doddle. Even the cabins were cleaner, and the pirates made her food!

Her daydreaming was cut short. Young Bert banged on the cabin door and told her to follow him up on deck. She promptly obeyed. She passed through the galleon, and male stenches mingled with the odours of rats, mice and other vermin, made her shudder. She realised why perfume was so important. On deck, she saw a sea of beady eyes, like rodents ready to pounce on their prey. This made Jimmelta slightly uncomfortable.

'Come here, Jimmelta,' said Captain Scurvvy, 'and have a bi' of this lava. Your ol' man has got Oli Gark to come in an' rescue you with his dangerous and deadly Svwat Team. This is puttin' us in a problem, 'cos we don't want to get mean or rott'n, but now... we 'ave to change...'

Jimmelta stared before sharply responding, 'I hope you're not going to be cruel to me and make me wash up or something. I am being a perfectly good prisoner, and I don't need to be stressed out...'

'STOP IT!' yelled Captain Scurvvy. 'We don' want to harm you, but OLI GARK! How much more dangerous can it be? We 'ave to do somethin'. So, this is wha' we plan to make Piggers pay up. Then we'll have some cash on top of this from Fred Slobberguts or wha' ever his name is at your television centre. We have to be harder now. D'you understand?' Jimmelta felt her blood run cold, her head pound and her eyes water.

'...So when you go down into the lava spills to get the marmalade lava, you then have to fill all the barrels with it an' roll 'em down the 'ills to the shore for the ship. You gonna get quite hot an' boffered, so we'll gives yous water, bu' no' sure 'bout food. Wha' d'you fink, men? Then you have to put the barrels on a small boat an' row to our Blackbird. Is this a problem Jimmelta?'

Jimmelta couldn't believe the change of heart. She felt angry at Oli Gark's men ruining her time with the pirates. The pirates looked at her sadly, as they had grown fond of her. They found it difficult to imagine her shovelling the sticky lava into barrels in this heat. Jimmelta slumped down on a sack and put her head in her hands and cried. All this was too much. She wanted to be happy again. Captain Scurvvy, quite choked up with emotion, got out his dirty handkerchief and wiped his eyes. The men had no choice.

'Loo', Jimmelta, this ain't easy for any of us, bu' we're left with no choice. Oli Gark, well, his Svwat Team are the terrors of the world for any causes, an' Gark's gone soft – mus' be the golden helicopters – an' 'e wants to help. We have to makes you appear to be sufferin'. The volcano will be righ' for this. An' you can be freed, an' we'll get some money to keep us 'appy. Simple really. Young Bert's in charge of you an' will take you tonigh' to a new place near the volcano on Marmalade island. So we 'ave new plans.'

The pirates knew the Svwat Team's power. Many were older and dreaded any contact with the formidable team.

That night, Jimmelta reluctantly slunk onto a rowing boat with her personal belongings and Young Bert. They headed for the caves in Marmalade Island. Young Bert stealthily rowed to the far bay, where the waters were slightly choppy and the air breezy. The cool air pleased Jimmelta. She looked and listened for any clues, an outline of her yacht, a familiar landmark, or, strains of laughter, or even the odd native war cry.

But nothing at all.

They rowed in silence, only the sound of the gentle waves accompanied them. Tears welled in her eyes.

Once in the bay, Young Bert eased the boat into a cave. Jimmelta was frightened. Young Bert, familiar with the location, jumped onto a rock and tied he boat. She shivered. The air was so cold, and icy, droplets of water dripped onto her head and trickled down her back. Actually, it felt cool and refreshing, but she wasn't in the mood to be positive: firstly, it was the depths of night; secondly, this was a serious kidnapping now; and thirdly, there was no light to put on her night creams. It was all too much now. She needed a warm soak in a diamond-encrusted bath, to regain her sense of happiness.

Young Bert sat on a rock, looked at his mobile and then said she should get some rest. Captain Scurvvy, convinced the team would not think Jimmelta was back on Marmalade Island, would search further a field. Young Bert wasn't quite so sure – all the information on the Svwat Team led him to believe, they would look everywhere. 'Look, Jimmelta, I thinks you should sleep now. We can't do anythin' till the mornin', and Capt'n Scurvvy is sure we will be fine. I will 'ave a nap too.'

Bert pounded his satchel into the shape

of a pillow on the edge of a rock, and immediately snuggled down on the damp f loor and went to sleep. Jimmelta sat upright, stared at the water, and wondered if she could escape or not. Swimming had never been high on the agenda in her life. How she regretted that now.

Soon Young Bert snored, the sound echoed and resounded like a whale. His tiny frame heaved up and down as he slept. She scanned the entrance of the cave, debated sneaking out, paddling, sticking to the shoreline. It appeared easy on television when people escaped. Then she noticed her luggage– her creams, shoes, outfits for each day of the kidnapping and, of course, her sun hat. She lay down, planned the escape in her mind. For the first time, she calculated different options to return home.

All this while Young Bert lay fast asleep. Soon Jimmelta fell asleep, upright, against her designer bags, the only reminder of her former life.

Chapter 21

Next morning she changed into her swimming costume, creamed herself, and laid out some clothes for the escape. Later Jimmelta sat on a rock with Young Bert, and gazed out at the bright blue day.

'So what are we doing today, Young Bert? I really am rather hungry, is there any food?'

Bert, stared ahead and stuffed cake into his mouth, and passed Jimmelta a piece, which disappeared quickly. He handed her some salami, crusty bread and a couple of tomatoes. Again she snatched them, ravenous from no food the previous night.

'Young Bert, are we just going to sit here all day and not do anything?' she continued in between mouthfuls of bread and salami.

He nodded. 'Fing is, Miss Jimmelta, we 'ave to be a little careful now. We 'ave the Svwat Team, an' we jus' 'ave to wait for Capt'n Scurvvy to tell us what's next. Bu' don' worry, I'll look after you. You're fine wif me. Just wait until Capt'n tells us.'

'Well, Bert –I think I'm going to leave the Young bit out, it just gets me so mad. Why don't we do something?' she responded to Bert, who was puzzled.

'What you wan' to do? P'raps a bi' of fishin'? I can show you how to fish...'

'No,' interrupted Jimmelta, 'no, I am thinking, I would so like to paddle and swim in the cave to keep fresh and cool. Would you, being so wonderful and strong, try to teach me how to swim I would like to do proper strokes. We can do this – just until we get our orders.'

Jimmelta smiled and gave Bert the famous Daily Chew glow she used to impress guests on her show. Before you could say Bob's your uncle, Bert coaxed Jimmelta into the water, and she used his arms as a f loat. Once in, she forgot her fear of creepy sea creatures. She paddled in the water with Bert by her side. He demonstrated how to kick her feet and swim the breast stroke. More than anything, Jimmelta was proud and not frightened. There were no sea monsters and crocodiles to eat her! Bert conveniently forgot to mention the sharks –even though a miniature sort in these shallows, they were still sharks. Jimmelta struggled to keep afloat. So Bert, keen to keep his prisoner occupied and happy, handed her an old f loat from the back of the boat.

'Come on, Jimmelta, 'old on t' the f loat and kick yer legs to keep swimmin'. Don' kep your mouth open, or you'll choke on the salt water. Come on, kick them legs.' Shocked at the firmness of his command, Jimmelta felt foolish – a rare event – and worked to master the skill. All this energy exhausted her, but

Young Bert, in his moment of power and mastery, instructed her to kick even harder and faster.

She couldn't muster a few words in case she gulped water and choked. Eventually, the actions became easier, and Jimmelta relaxed in the water. Even though it was dark and chilly in the cave, the water was warm and it soothed her.

As time passed, Jimmelta swam cautiously in the cave, keeping close to the boulders and rocks. Young Bert, now bored, talked on his mobile. She felt cocooned, hidden from the world, and, for a few moments forgot she was a hostage. Deep in the cave, Jimmelta never heard the golden helicopters circle the island.

Back on Marmalade Island at first light, Oli Gark summoned his Svwat team, who, after a late night with the Rindulees, were bright, sparkling, and ready for action. The children watched intently as the team stood on the beach, listening to their instructions by their calculating leader. Piggers, The Tank and the Inherited Australian Convicts observed.

'So men, we findz Jimmelta today and make our Piggerz 'appy. Youz know whatz to do.'

The team saluted Oli, and at the next instruction, got into the helicopters, which spun high in the sky and disappeared from view.

'Aw, I'd love to be part of tha', gettin' our

Jimmelta,' said Pinky Squat, as he waved at the spectacle in the sky. Then he returned to his chores on the Jimmi Chew. Piggers stood on the deck and watched intently as the team dispersed. His conversations with Oli Gark had resulted in an excellent plan to rescue his darling Doughy, without hurting the pirates. Oli, on the other hand, thought Piggers too kind.

From the other side of the deck The Tank shouted to the children. 'We have work to do. Whilst the amazing Svwat Team rescue your mother, you need to get on with your lessons.' She yelled and they followed her. Piggers ignored the children got out his mobile and dialled a number. They slouched away behind The Tank, once again, their formidable and powerful tutor.

'We need to put the plan into action,' murmured Paisley to Gingham, as he sat down in the classroom. Polka sulked when told to open her books. The other two stared at their desks.

'We should wait to see what happens to our mother,'muttered Polka. Her eyes gleamed with hatred towards The Tank, who set out work for the children to complete.

'Now look, Polka, I am thinking about your mother all the time, but we must do something until we have any news. I know you would rather stay with your father, but he's busy working with Oli Gark to get her rescued.' The Tank's comment was reasonable, so to help their father, the children obeyed her instructions .

Whilst quiet on the Jimmi Chew, the Svwat Team scoured the area, their golden helicopters, equipped for the most dangerous situations. The team eyed the islands. There was no sign of The Blackbird, it was safely tucked away. The helicopters flew closely over each of the islands, but the crews couldn't see any pirates or clues to Jimmelta's whereabouts.

Away from Marmalade Island hidden in a cave, Captain Scurvvy heard the propellers of the gleaming monsters above in the sky. He sat quietly, and hoped they would hover somewhere else.

'Look, men, we have to get away from The Blackbird, or take the masts down and sail her to another island at night.'

The men stared at their leader, who appeared fearless. Though secretly, Young Bert's information about the Svwat Team petrified him. He wished he had not kidnapped Jimmelta. The men, worn from a tough existence on the seas, were not fit, and many wanted a peaceful retirement. Captain Scurvvy regretted the kidnapping now, as it put the lives of his men in jeopardy.

'Capt'n, we goona do wha'ever yous wish,' replied one of the older pirates. 'Jus' let us know wha' and we'll follow.' The men nodded in agreement. Captain Scurvvy listened to the drone of the propellers. The noise echoed and resounded in the cave and deafened everybody.

After the helicopters left, Captain Scurvvy phoned Young Bert and discussed when to move Jimmelta to the volcano. Young Bert wasn't so sure Jimmelta was going to do this. He watched her swim on her front with the float quite confidently. He doubted if Jimmelta would obey, and trudge up the side of the volcano to fill barrels. Jimmelta didn't hear a word Young Bert said, and focused on improving her swimming skills. The water was so warm, it reminded her of permanently hot baths at home – without the bubbles.

After the conversation, Young Bert relaxed and watched Jimmelta slowly, with great determination, swim around the perimeter of the black cave. The pocket of blue sky at the entrance gave a window of warmth and life.

Back at the island after a whole day, the Svwat Team discussed the lack of progress with Oli Gark. He wasn't amused they hadn't caught the pirates, or rescued Jimmelta. Gark banged his fists on the side of a golden helicopters and snarled at his men. They made him look a fool!

The children, finished with lessons sat on the sand besides Piggers, and waited for news. The Tank, stood on the deck, with her binoculars, staring in all directions, to glean any clues which would help.

But she saw nothing.

There was just an empty ocean in all directions, not even a boat on the horizon.

Nothing but sun, sand and a vast, vast sea. Yells and splurts of rage from Oli Gark, indicated the team had not rescued Jimmelta.

For the first time since the team's arrival, the children cried. Oli, impatient at the best of times, shouted at them to be quiet and not so weak. Piggers turned to comfort the children, then quietly ushered them towards the yacht. They slunk behind their father, heads bowed, deflated.

Once gone, Oli furious with his men, ordered them to search the area again. Dejected, they went again, recharged by Oli Gark's dreadful temper, and the family's disappointment.

Hidden in another cave Jimmelta swam around the perimeter of the cave. She hummed and imagined she was getting strong. This swimming lark was such a good idea! All she needed now, was a clean towel from the Church of Harvey Nichols. She swam all day, and never stopped for a drink or something to eat. Young Bert saw his hostage quiet and focused. Normally, she complained of boredom, but now she was remarkably engrossed.

The day wore on and the sun began to set, Young Bert reluctantly nodded off to sleep. He still waited for instructions to take Jimmelta to the top of the volcano, and didn't relish it at all. On The Blackbird, the pirates, thought the Svwat Team might discover their hideout. They searched the galleon for ammunition, but only salvaged some old cannons used to target empty tin cans. Captain Scurvvy doubted their use. So as the sun set, they heard the boom of the helicopters swirling overhead. The Salami pirates sat glumly, devising ways to defend themselves. Old Triggers, finally said, 'Wha'about usin' the barrels of sticky lava in the catapults an' aiming it at the engines? We're all good shots, an' while we won't win, we can give it a goo' try!'

At first, the pirates smirked and sniggered at Old Triggers, who everyone agreed, was mad at times. However, Captain Scurvvy, desperate to to defend his galleon and men, shushed everyone while Triggers explained his plan. Nodding in agreement, the captain visualised the lava clogging the engines.

Better still, if the helicopters were lured to the mouth of the cave.

'Men, this could work, an' we could jus' give Jimmelta back withou' any trouble. What d'ya say?'

Cheers from the pirates gave Captain Scurvvy's the answer he needed. So they laid a trap for the world's most powerful team. Barrels of sticky lava appeared on the deck, along with leftover gunpowder from previous exploits. The men gathered the lava balls, rolled in gunpowder, ready to fire if the choppers attempted the entrance of the cave. The pirates were not going to lose without a fight. They worked into the night, and used the valuable stock of sticky lava for cannon balls. Once done, they surveyed the huge mound with pride. Old Triggers smiled, convinced the strategy would surprise Gark's team.

Captain Scurvvy was still concerned they couldn't defend themselves if the Svwat Team raided The Blackbird. Capturing the pirates was his worst nightmare. He couldn't let his pirates, his friends suffer!

Chapter 22

Back on the yacht the evidence looked bleak. The Mini Rindulees huddled on the deck and waited for something to happen.

Pinky Squat attempted to entertain the children, but they didn't notice. Their favourite food was left untouched. The Tank, quieter than normal, gazed out to sea and wished Jimmelta was home.

Poor Marjory and Jimmy John, still not

allowed to film the events, spent their time phoning Fred Slobbretto with news. He was delighted Oli Gark's team planned a rescue. The evening drew to a close and the children stayed up, but after a while retreated to bed exhausted.

The Tank couldn't sleep. She wanted it all to end. She wanted Jimmelta back so her young pupils could regain their excitement for life.

Gingham hatched a plan with Polka and Paisley. They intended to take a canoe, and find Jimmelta. The children had no idea where she was.

'We can't just sit here can we? Let's row out and follow the shoreline and look in the other caves.' The others nodded in agreement.

'But how will we know that she's not hundreds of miles away? We can't be sure we'll see her. The pirates will want to make sure she's hidden, perhaps chained up,' added Paisley.

'Yeah, but it's better to do something rather than sit around worrying like mad. At least we know the Salami pirates have been fine with her, and she did sound sort of alright when she spoke,' said Polka. 'I'm not sure this will work, but once we get a canoe, we can sneak off and find her. We'll see what happens,' Paisley gulped as he spoke. He missed his mother. They gathered a torch, binoculars, bottles of water, a towel and a jumpers, in case it turned cooler.

Once it was quiet, the children sneaked

off the yacht to one of the canoes on the beach. Stealthily as they could, they pushed it out to sea, jumped on it, and rowed to their left keeping near the shoreline. Not used to the weight of the oars, initially made the rowing a little slow.

Once further out, Polka and Gingham rowed and guided canoe, while Paisley scoured the area with the binoculars looking for any clues. It was difficult as everything was black, and the only light was the moon high in the sky. They headed towards the entrances of caves, but couldn't see anything.

'I don't think we'll ever find her,' said Paisley, to the others.

'Well, at least we're doing something.

She is our mother,' responded Polka.

'We'll just keep looking,' added Gingham. They continued their search. The first cave they entered was small, the mouth of it was low and narrow. The children crouched as they entered, using the oars against the cave walls to balance the canoe. Gingham yelled out for his mother, which echoed round the cave. They all sat motionless. They couldn't hear a sound.

Sure she wasn't in this cave, Polka and Gingham rowed out, back into the open water. 'Well, I'm glad to get out of there,' she said, 'I found it so cramped and felt a little frightened.'

Back on the yacht, The Tank decided to have a midnight adventure on the island (without the children, of course) to pass the time. She asked Marjory's to join her on a, 'Tank Midnight Adventure.'

'Oh, what a fun idea,' said Marjory, 'amongst all the horror of Jimmelta's kidnapping. How wonderful! And, we can have Jimmy John film while we have the fun and action!'

Marjory, phoned Jimmy John, and with the camera hidden, under a large loose shirt, he joined them. Marjory quickly dressed. She put on light trousers, a long sleeved shirt, and slid a lipstick and tube of cream in her back pocket, plus a comb, mascara, perfume: then stood ready to go.

'D'you want to bring your rollers and face pack as well?' snarled The Tank, her hands on her huge hips. Marjory ignored the sarcastic remark.

Jimmy John raced behind the women, down the beach towards the mountains.

'Shouldn't we have a torch or something?' he gasped, lugging the equipment as he rushed to keep up. The Tank turned to face him and presented a torch out of her back pocket. They walked to the edge of the forest, dense with trees and foliage and with each step, climbed the mountain.

'I think we should turn back and follow the coastline. That's far better to film and much safer,' commented Marjory, not convinced The Tank knew where she was going.

Jimmy John, exhausted from carrying

camera, added, 'Yeah, I'll stay on the beach and get some great shots for the viewers back home.'

The Tank agreed, so they descended the mountain. Marjory constantly flicked insects off her skin and squashed them.

The sea was a pleasant relief and both women. Though fully clothed, they swam, hoping the salt water numbed the countless insect bites. The moon covered the sky and illuminated Marmalade Island, so the landscape looked like an array of silhouettes.

Jimmy John filmed as the women strode though the gentle waves, The Tank used a thick broken branch to test the ground ahead, preventing unpleasant surprises.

After sometime, Jimmy John shouted he needed to sit and have a rest. The Tank held the camera while he swam to refresh, the air was hot and humid.

The adventure was a positive experience for the group as they exchanged stories about the family. They covered a range of topics, working with Jimmelta, feeling sorry for Piggers, making the children work, and the Inherited Australian Convicts. Time passed and they sat on boulders by the shore and discussed the pirates' fate.

Marjory glanced out to sea and stared. She noticed movement in the water and asked for the torch. Although difficult to see any detail, the outline resembled three people in a canoe. She beamed the light steadily, and said to the others, 'I think we have company. I think the children are out on a canoe...'

'Impossible they all went to bed. I saw them go.' said The Tank firmly. 'Here, let me have look.' She grabbed the torch.. 'I recognise them, that's Gingham rowing.' She yelled out their names. At first, the children ignored her, but Polka said there was no point. They yelled they wanted to find their mother and bring her back home to the yacht. The Tank yelled and beckoned the group to join their search.

The children rowed to the group. 'Come here you lot,' The Tank said gently, 'we'll all find your mother together. It looks great this canoe, and it's useful getting in and out of the caves around Marmalade Island.' The children couldn't believe her kindness. So both groups joined forces to find Jimmelta.

They searched the waters around the island. The Tank, convinced Jimmelta wouldn't be too far away, kept these thoughts to herself.

Chapter 23

Still hostage in the cave, the next day Jimmelta paddled in the deep blue, warm water determined to master the swimming skills. The sun was high in the sky and everything was so bright outside. Finally, after teaching Jimmelta to have more confidence with her swimming, Young Bert snuggled up against a rock facing the wall of the cave. Bored with waiting for instructions from his captain, he fell asleep and snored loudly. It echoed in the hollow space like a small earthquake. She glanced at him hunched on a rumpled jacket, then her eyes riveted on a small oblong shape, and realised it was a mobile. Quietly as possible, Jimmelta swam towards it. She heaved her aching arms onto a nearby boulder and grabbed the phone. Then she slid back into the water with her float and kicked silently towards the mouth of the cave. She clutched onto the mobile and debated whether she should keep it or not. Once she realised a wet mobile was useless, Jimmelta threw it as far as possible.

Jimmelta, wistfully turned, and sadly surveyed her beautifully, packed, captive luggage, (no longer needed), and swam to the entrance. Her hat and sunglasses plonked on, with lip balm clenched in the palm of her hand, she peered right and left, gripped tightly to the float, and sidled out of the cave. She needed to escape before Young Bert realised, but had no idea where she was on the island. She hoped Stickiano was to the right, so angled herself to the left and kept close to the perimeter of the island.

Every kick left her a little more exhausted, but also a little less fearful. The water lapped and cooled her skin and hair in the scorching heat. Every now and then Jimmelta turned to check if Young Bert was behind. She half-expected him to appear in the rowing boat and haul her back to the cave. This filled her with alarm. Once aware of her escape, she knew Captain Scurvvy would make life terrible for the family.

The waves lulled her to sheer cliffs so the float doubled as a form of protection, against shards   of rock. As the sun lowered in the sky, Jimmelta wondered how far she could swim, before reaching a beach of any kind. As the moon rose and sun slipped from the horizon, she was alarmed by strange, wild noises from the island. Determined to concentrate, and use the cliffs as a guide, she continued her escape. Her legs struggled to maintain any speed, while the lower muscles in her back burnt with pain. Her sore finger tips were numb, and gripping the float was painful. All these factors resulted in a slow, arduous swim.

However, she had no choice.

She was hungry, thirsty and desperately wanted to rest and perhaps sleep. Then she saw it, the first signs of sand, just the smallest boulder all in a bay.

Her first sand.

The continual vertical cliff face now slithered into a bay. She swam along the shoreline she saw the bay - deserted and safe. But it wasn't the one where the Jimmi Chew was anchored.

Jimmelta limped ashore, hungry, with chapped lips, and slumped onto a boulder to rest. Although it wasn't cold, she shivered, her teeth chattered as she took stock of the surroundings. Later, after a rest, she forced herself to walk across the soft sand, which caressed her feet. She squinted her eyes, and examined the bay intently, to gauge where she was. And she was hungry! She wondered if any fruit or coconuts lay on the beach, to eat. It was difficult to see in the moonlight, but she bent on her knees, and patted the sand, to feel what was there.

She touched what seemed to be a banana, held it up to the moonlight and recognised the outline. Grabbing the skin, she peeled it and plunged the soft, sweet, succulent fruit into her mouth. The banana seeped through the crevices of her teeth, soothed her gums, massaged her tongue, and slipped smoothly down her throat.

Once finished, she grappled on the beach for more bananas, desperate to continue the quest for delicious fruit. Finally, she found a pile of moon shaped fruits. She held them up in the sky and cried with joy. She fumbled, and tore open the skin of each banana. She grasped the pulpy, creamy, fruit, and squeezed them like toothpaste into her mouth. Each squirted out of its skin, and she shovelled the food as quickly as she could. This continued until no longer hungry and her appetite was sated. Jimmelta mentally prepared to swim to the next bay. Even though she was full, her body was depleted of energy, and her eyes, though shielded by glasses, were sore and hot.

The thought of swimming to the next bay made her feel weak and sick. Once back in the water, feebly she kicked her legs, each movement pained, and she held the float close to her chest as a support. Turning to the next bay, Jimmelta saw lights shimmering in the distance. She knew these were from the Jimmi Chew.

Joy fuelled her body, to swim towards the huge silhouette at the end of the bay. Her arms didn't feel leaden anymore, and she didn't notice the soreness of her lips, thighs, or hands, as fervently swam to the nearest point on the shore. The water seemed to go on forever and she kicked as hard   as she could to get to the next bay. The yacht appeared so close and yet so far away. The sight of the lights twinkling in the distance made Jimmelta cry a little, as she thought of the children and Piggers. With this picture entrenched in her mind, she was determined to make it back home.

She swam limply, every movement of her legs and arms seemed to be weighed down. As she approached the shore, the lights on the yacht became a little clearer. Jimmelta smiled she was on her way back home.

As her feet sank into the first sand in the bay, Jimmelta cried. The yacht stood clearly at the farthest point of the bay. The moon displayed it like a proud parent for all to see. She finally reached the shore, stumbled to the sand, caught her breath, and scoured the bay, determined not to fall asleep.

She was nearly home.

The distant sound of voices alerted

Jimmelta, ones she recognised but couldn't place. She blinked and noted small silhouettes, like moving pinpricks walking in the shore. Then she heard The Tank booming at the group. She stood up, yelled loudly 'It's me! HELP!! it's me!

Jimeltaaaaaaaaaaaaaaaaaaaaa a a Heeeeeelllllllllppppppp'

The group ran toward the screaming, until they saw Jimmelta's outline stumbling and crying.

It all went blank for Jimmelta. Her final memory before collapsing was the image of Polka and Marjory in tears.

Everything was a blur.

Jimmelata, against all odds, had escaped the Salami pirates. Better still, Jimmy

John had the rescue on film, and knew this incredible coverage was excellent for the ratings. Ahh, mused Marjory, this wonderful ending to Jimmelta's kidnapping ensured top position for the chat show.

And Jimmelta was home!!

Chapter 24

Marjory goggled in disbelief, at a limp and exhausted Jimmelta who collapsed into her arms, and rambled incoherently. Marjory struggled to hold her and asked for help. 'Look, I can't hold her! Can somebody help?' The Tank, equipped for any event, scooped Jimmelta in her arms and walked towards the Jimmi Chew. Marjory and the three children ran behind screaming with excitement. Jimmy John, stunned by the appearance of Jimmelta, and the reunion with Gingham, Paisley and Polka, filmed as much as possible.

They waded through the waters, and shouted to draw attention. They approached and the Svwat Team lined up on the beach by the golden helicopters. They turned to the figures, aware The Tank carried a body. The men disbanded and surrounded the group, still unable to comprehend the situation. Marjory, determined to tell the team, nudged in front of The Tank and explained:

'We were walking along the shoreline, you know, getting a bit of fresh air, wanting to get away from all the pressure. We saw the children on a canoe searching for their mother so they joined us. Well, as we searched the bay, looking for Jimmelta and we just heard some screeching and didn't know who, or what it was. Then, we saw the outline of a figure stumbling towards us, screaming out her name! We recognised the name and knew it was Jimmelta!'

The men unable to comprehend the language, still understood the excitement. They worked out, this was Jimmelta, and were amazed she had escaped all on her own. AND without their help. They envisaged Oli Gark's fury and dreaded his reaction to the news.

Once told, Piggers was thrilled. To have his beautiful Doughy back after this terrible experience, was a dream. He, like everyone else was astounded at Jimmelta's had cunning escape.

Although nobody knew the details of her route back to safety, they acknowledged her incredible bravery. More so, since she disliked swimming.

Piggers thanked the fortitude of his wonderful children, the group, Marjory, Jimmy John and of course, The Tank. She wanted Jimmelta back on the Jimmi Chew for a warm bath and a rest and mentioned this to Piggers. This tender behaviour touched Piggers.

The Tank carried Jimmelta to her quarters Piggers trailed behind. He was thrilled to see his wife again.

After several hours sleep Jimmelta woke up, squinted, and scanned her golden bedroom. The fluffiness of the duvet snuggled her shivering body, and relaxed her. Scented candles wafted aromas to soothed her. 'I think I must have made it home,' she muttered, still confused. Any muscle movement was painful. She felt shattered and numb with exhaustion. Her lips were dry and chapped. It was painful to move her mouth. She knew she was safe: safe with the family, her children and, her beloved Piggers.

'Oh, JIMMELTA! How we've missed you and how worried we've been about you,' whispered Piggers between tears and gulps. 'We have a wonderful warm bubble bath ready for you. And, your favourite soaps and creams. And from Harvey Nichols, warm, scented towels and soft, soft nightclothes!' Piggers added. She opened her eyes fully and smiled. Perhaps it was a dream, though her body ached.

'OH, MY DARLING PIGGERS, I AM HOME!' she said loudly, and kissed his forehead.

'We must, my love, get you into a nice, warm bath.'

Piggers helped her out of bed. She gingerly and carefully edged towards her beautiful golden bathroom, where the aromas of vanilla and jasmine candles filled the room. Once in the perfectly heated bath, she sank into the creamy, silky, pink bubbles, all from the Church of Harvey Nichols...

She smiled.

She was valiant escaping the pirates.

She was an intrepid explorer!

She was a heroine!

She was home!

Piggers, quietly vowed never to let his beloved Doughy out of his sight again.

The Inherited Australian Convicts amazed at everything – wondered what the team planned for the pirates.

King Rindulee and the Mini Rindulees promoted Jimmelta to the status of a goddess. So they decided to build a shrine to her on the beach, not of gold, but native wood and stone. As the natives collected their materials, King Rindulee also added another new title making her, Jimmelta, Queen of Marmalade Island. Now she was a goddess and a queen!

Relieved the ransom was no longer needed, Fred Slobbretto knew the programme's ratings to be highest ever. He chuckled to himself as he lit a huge cigar, and put his feet on his desk. He glanced back and forth between news coverage of Jimmelta's escape on all channels, and compared them to The Daily Chew, hosted by Marjory Stickle Swamp Stick. His job was safe, nothing else mattered.

The doorman outside the television studios, Big Diddy, shocked lost his bet on Fred Slobbretto being demoted. However, after interviews with the media, Big Diddy's touch with fame, cemented an unearthed desire to work in television. He visualized a role presenting the news, or even a chat show, and thought his people skills working on the doors excellent.

After bathing for ages, Jimmelta slowly dried, as her body ached so much. She dusted down with specially scented talcum powder, and put on clean, perfectly ironed nightclothes. She padded back to bed, fell back onto a cloud of scented pillows, so light, she felt she was f loating. Once again, she drifted off to sleep. She was in clean sheets, smelt beautiful, and back in her own bed. She was free from rats, dead creatures, dirt, grease, slime and stale, stinking, rotting food. Piggers held her hand, as her eyelids became heavy, like lead. She finally went to sleep, and he sat by the bed, joyous at her return.

While she slept, reporters went crazy. All wanted an interview with the family, her servants, The Tank, the Svwat Team – in fact anybody linked to her. The commotion below on the beach was staggering. The children, now heroes, watched as countless people land by boat or helicopter. They realised the importance of this event globally. They stood close to The Tank and the Inherited Australian Convicts, overwhelmed at everything.

Jimmelta slept on through all of this.

Hours later, unaware of the commotion, she woke in her luxurious bed, the white, silk duvet snuggled gently around her body.

Meanwhile, the Svwat Team hunted down the Salami pirates determined to bring them to the yacht. Oli Gark was determined to bring them to justice. But Piggers, not aggressive, insisted he scrutinized the Salami pirates, before he summoned the police. He wished to see Jimmelta's kidnapper's. Reluctantly, Oli informed his team, equally unimpressed at the decision, to capture, but not torture the pirates.

Of course, Marjory and Jimmy John basked in worldwide attention from the media. They gave interviews about the family and of course, the incredible rescue. The children, feted for their courageous efforts to find Jimmelta, enjoyed the praise and attention too. Coverage across the globe was exceptional, and Jimmelta's escape was viral on the Internet. So much praise and popularity!

She received congratulations from the Queen, delighted Jimmelta was safe, and was invited for 'a cup of tea to catch up on all the gossip'! More surprisingly, the handbag shaped yacht was now in every paper in the western hemisphere. Shipbuilders keen to copy the style, now insisted the design to be the most popular for clients. Jimmelta was once again, one of the most popular women in the world.

Chapter 25

The Svwat Team hovered above the shores around Ambergris Caye. The helicopters tried to nudge into every cave entrance. The team bellowed out through a loudspeaker demanding the Salami pirates give themselves up.

'COMEZ OUT NOWZ! WE KNOWZ YOUZ ARE THERE!'

The blaring sound from the loudspeakers,

reverberated through each cave. Hidden deep within one of them, his ship's sails pulled down as far as they could go, Captain Scurvvy surveyed his men. The loudspeakers boomed in all directions on the island, and he knew something had gone wrong. He was worried, very worried, for his men who sat petrified. This really wasn't how it was meant to turn out.

Captain Scurvvy hoped Jimmelta was safe. He wanted to give her back to Piggers. Try as he might, he couldn't reach Young Bert on the phone. Where was Young Bert? He had no idea if he was safe. He worried because supplies were low, especially of clean water. He also knew he had every right to be worried, since the Svwat Team intended to find the pirates.

Suddenly, a light shone into the cave. The men were motionless, hoping it would disappear. It circled the perimeter of the lagoon, in which The Blackbird looked like a long black boulder against the creviced rocks. The light shone onto the galleon. The men froze as it beamed onto the deck. Inch by inch, it covered it in a blaze, vividly showing every plank, barrel, can, folded mast, sack, rope and gun. The pirates, along with Captain Scurvvy, cowered below deck, hardly breathing in case this was detected. The beam settled on the deck and continued to circumnavigate it, trying to work out to whom the vessel belonged.

Suddenly, the men heard a huge, booming

Russian voice at the mouth of the cave. Below deck, the men prayed it would go away, but it grew nearer and nearer:

'CAPTAIN SCURVVY, WE HAVE TO TELLZ YOUZ WE HAVE JIMMELTA! SHE ESCAPEDZ! HA! HA! HA! I AM ZE OLI GARK! MY MEN WILLZ CAPTURE YOUZ NOW.' The voice went very quiet. 'AND PIGGERS IS SO NICE, AND WANTZ YOU SAFE AND ALIVE ! IF IT WAZ ME, I WOULD HAVE YOUZ BEGGING FOR YOUR LIVEZ.

– BUT PIGGERS IZ NICE! COME OUT NOW! All OF YOUZ!'

Oli Gark's snazzy mini submarine slithered beneath the water to the side of The Blackbird – right next to it!

The Salami pirates huddled together. They all knew Oli's dangerous and formidable reputation, and worried what his team might do. The galleon shook with the movement of footsteps, as men climbed onto the deck. Not just one or two footsteps –there seemed to be swarms of men pounding up above. Captain Scurvvy stood up as the footsteps reached the door.

Everyone was quiet.

Everyone was still.

Everyone stared ahead at the door.

It swung open, banged against the wall and rattled. The Svwat Team stood in line, ready to enter. The first in the team was so huge his biceps touched either side of the door frame. They walked in, encircled the

Salami pirates, who steeled themselves. The Svwat Team stood, emotionless and ready for their commander to make his entrance.

Oli Gark, walked in and sat down at the long table and inspected the pirates. His arms folded, announced his intentions to take them to the yacht. His team led them out. The pirates glanced at each other confused. The team pointed the dispirited pirates towards rowing boats, now waiting alongside the galleon. Nobody spoke. Captain Scurvvy prayed a conversation with Piggers might be worthwhile.

The trip back to Marmalade Island was subdued. The pirates were agitated about their future, once dismissed by Piggers. Nobody thought about Young Bert, still in the cave, on Marmalade Island, still distraught at Jimmelta's escape.

Once on shore, the pirates rounded up, trudged led to the golden yacht. Here, Piggers and a refreshed Jimmelta waited for them. The Inherited Australian Convicts and The Tank stood with their arms folded, and their faces thunderous. Jimmy John followed the walk to their escaped hostage, each pirate bedraggled and limping. The children cried at the sight, and clung to their mother, who felt strangely calm.

Almost serene.

She was home with her beautiful family and everything was now in place.

'Come here, you dreadful lot!' thundered Piggers. He roared as the Salami pirates faced their punishment.

'To be fair, Piggers,' said Jimmelta, 'the pirates were very nice to me. It all turned nasty when Oli Gark turned up with his golden helicopters. However, I was getting tired of dirty clothes and smelly conditions. And, I did miss my scented candles. Bert, where is he?' Jimmelta scanned the deck and the pirates, who said nothing.

Captain Scurvvy cleared his throat and whispered, 'I don't know. I would just like to say we nev'r had any intention of hurtin' Jimmelta and all liked her very much on board.' The pirates nodded at this.

'I knows wha' we did was wron', bu' we wouldn' have hurt her for the world – would we, men?' The pirates nodded in agreement.

'This is King Rindulee's island and he has the power to decide your fate. It's up to him,' Piggers replied.

King Rindulee grimaced and said, 'I think we're going to make you our slaves to work at the edge of our volcano. You will gather the Marmaladian lava to export to other countries. Captain Scurvvy, if any of your men try to escape, we'll take your bad deeds to the police. They will make your lives a misery.' The pirates smiled, relieved by this and nodded. Jimmelta and Piggers pleased at the decision, relaxed slightly, and Oli Gark sulked.

At this point, Young Bert, found in a cave on the other side of the island, skulked on to the deck.

Ah! All this on camera, smirked Marjory, as the pirates accepted their destiny. Peering up, she spotted Jimmelta laughing at the captured men.

In the coming weeks, viewers tuned into the pirates new lives. They worked on the sides of the volcano, filling barrels with Marmaladian lava and supported the natives. It wasn't too bad at all. Captain Scurvvy still their leader, planned to build a school for the native children. The Tank, after some thought, decided stay and teach on the island. Although fond of the family, she wanted to be useful on the island. Besides, she loved swimming in the hot sea.

Once Jimmelta fully recovered from her exploits, Oli Gark's team flew the family to a larger island. From there, they jetted back to England to their wonderful home, Bullion Castle. The sensational story made headlines all over the world, and everyone clambered to try to speak to Jimmelta. Piggers, so thrilled to see his beloved Doughy home safely, he announced a National Jimmelta Day and paid for children in every school to have a treat: a delicious doughnut.

Of course, Jimmelta's hat was no longer a joke. Everyone now clambered to have a tractor hat designed for special occasions. And the handbag shaped yacht, was a dream for anyone wanting to copy her style: though, obviously not in gold. Better still, the Jimmi Chew was moored in a wide wharf off the Thames. It had a special viewing gallery for visitors to take photos of it. The handbag anchored firmly, in the wharf, glistened and gleamed in the sunlight as a new beacon of hope.

The children went back to school heroes, and (strangely enough), were happy to work hard. Everything appeared simple after The Tank's tutoring!

The Inherited Australian Convicts, well, they returned to sorting out life in Bullion Castle. Life without The Tank, was tranquil!

Jimmelta arrived at the studio every day to swarms of fans, desperate for an autograph. She waved as she entered television centre. She acknowledged the crowds, beaming with happiness. Then she routinely stuffed half a doughnut into her mouth, as lava dribbled down the side of her chin. She stuck out her tongue and scooped it up, and smacked her lips in delight. This always thrilled the hordes of fans each day.

Now, she was always flanked by Jimmy John and Marjory. Big Diddy became her personal door man at the studio, and loved working for his heroine. Fred Slobbretto worshipped Jimmelta and listened intently to all her ' excellent and intelligent ideas.'

Life indeed was perfect.

Everybody loved her. Well, for the moment anyway!

The Idiot Family on Holiday

The Idiot Family on Holiday is a great children's adventure that even adults can enjoy with their children. Although this is aimed at for children between 9 to11years, I and my 4-year-old niece read it together. She quite enjoyed the pirates and the Piggers characters. This a great adventure story but also it had themes children and parent could talk about within the story which I think would make learning fun for children

The story itself follows Jimmelta and her husband Piggers as they try and get their gold handbag shaped yacht into the water and moved by royal demand. Jimmelta sees this as the perfect opportunity to take her children on holiday, but to do that she needs to find them a tutor and the search begins. Will the handbag shaped yacht get into the water? Will the children's tutor be more than they can handle? And how much adventure can one handbag shaped yacht cause? You should read this book to find out.

I thought the characters were funny and likable. I even liked Jimmelta although sometimes she comes across very self-motivated. But this makes her story arc very strong because we see her grow throughout the adventure, and each new person she meets shapes her in some ways.

I also like Piggers because he clearly loves his wife and would do anything for her. I think he teaches children to give time and patience to family members, even if their dreams are a bit extreme or there are embracing moments, support and love goes a long way.

I also thought chapter size in this book was long enough for the age range and can be read at bedtime in stages. This book is very entertaining and would keep children guessing right up until the end. Reading aloud how pirates speak will make them laugh – It did make my niece Roseanna laugh.

Children love deep adventure books, packed with interesting characters and some little fun lessons along the way. This book also has a great ending any child will be happy with.

'Four-year-old Roseanna's thoughts were: Piggers is a funny name. I like jam and can she get her bag to float like the handbag yacht. Pirates go ahhhh! And she's glad her family is not an Idiot Family lol'

Katrina Hart,
Author of *Finding Destiny*

The Idiot Family on Holiday

This has to be one of those fantastical reads! I'd say the pitch is a reader who loves something escapist and wacky. It is an adventure story and it is also a modern tale set in modern times!

Readers will need to be fluent and able to 'get' the constant puns littered throughout this story and an awareness of London culture may need to be a pre-requisite too.

Jimmelta – the main character is initially introduced to us as decidedly irritating however you cannot fail to love her by the end of the story. Her doggedly loyal husband Piggers must win the prize for blind love and loyalty given the challenges she presents to him.

The children's tutor nicknamed The Tank has more than a Mary Poppins firm but fair element to her.

In terms of the baddies within this narrative there cannot be many stories containing both pirates, Inherited Australian convicts and a Russian Billionnaire. However they are all bathed in a warm glow by the end of the story which seems to end well for all.

I can't help but feel this would be the perfect escapist read for Year 6 post their national tests in June- a wacky and fantastical read for pure fun!

**Sally Rundell,
International Education Consultant**